DEATH OF A DANCING MASTER

For Carol ~ who
dances through time

M.E. KEMP

with energy & grace!

M. E. Kemp

L & L Dreamspell
Spring, Texas

ISBN: 978-1-60318-240-9

Library of Congress Control Number: 2010936417

Visit us on the web at www.lldreamspell.com

Published by L & L Dreamspell
Printed in the United States of America

To my husband, Jack Rothstein, for his unfailing support and to Emily, the Matriarch of the family.

PROLOGUE

Boston, 1693

The young man knocked but no one opened the door to him. Thinking that perhaps his knock was too timid, he balled up his fist and banged. Still there was no response. Evidently the gentleman was too occupied to hear. Perkney said he had an appointment, but the young man assumed Perkney said it in an effort to get rid of him. No matter, the young man felt it his duty to tender an apology for his intemperate words, and apologize he would. He thrust open the door and walked into the long room.

Seeing no one he called out, "Perkney, are you there?" And repeated, "Perkney?" He took two steps forward.

Although the room was one long space, it was divided into three sections, the first being a small antechamber where Perkney greeted guests. There was a round table to the right, with paper, a quill, an inkpot and a silver tray for calling cards upon it. A narrow chair sat next to the table. To his left the wall held hooks for coats and cloaks. Beneath the hooks a small rug covered the floor, with a bootjack for removing muddy footwear. Perkney was quite particular about his guests removing their muddy clogs or boots.

The next section of the room flickered with candles in wall sconces. The candles illuminated wall hangings of bewigged ladies and gentlemen lounging in country gardens. Two gilded armchairs were placed against the wall. Across the room a wooden stool served as a seat for the fiddler, who doubled as Perkney's servant.

The last section was left in gloom, a bare pine floor where the dancing master gave lessons in sword-play. The young man remembered a pile of foils against the wall but he could not quite make out the stack from his position across the room. Nor could he see the door that led to Perkney's private rooms. Perhaps Perkney was asleep in there.

The young man called out across the space: "It's me, Perkney. Jacob Joyliffe. I've come back to apologize to you." His words hung unanswered in the late afternoon air. Joyliffe felt a sense of oppression. Where was the man? He'd left the dancing master for no more than twenty minutes, if that. Perkney hadn't appeared to be going out. He'd said he had an appointment. Joyliffe assumed the appointment was a lesson of some sort. The man taught fencing as well as ungodly dance.

"Perkney?" Really, this was too much. The man must be avoiding him. Here he'd rushed back because conscience scolded him for his rash words to the dancing master and the man hid from him like a naughty child. He'd hurried back on purpose so he would not interrupt the man's lessons, even if he could not approve of the lascivious movement. Court dances. Just because the wicked Louis of France did them, there was no reason for Godly Protestants to mimic the Papist King's example.

There was nothing for it but to cross the room and make himself known at the door to Perkney's rooms. The thought that Perkney might not be asleep there—he might possibly be engaged in wanton behavior—made him wince, but his conscience would not allow him to hesitate. It was his duty to apologize to the dancing master. He straightened his shoulders and strode across the space.

"Perkney. Mr. Perkney, it's me, Jacob Joyliffe." He called out a warning. Frustrated he pounded upon the door.

"Perkney, I know you're in there. Wake up, Man. I have come to apologize to you." He waited. "Perkney?" He knocked to no avail. Frustrated, he turned. The dancing master was arrogant, as he had cause to believe, but he hadn't thought the man a coward.

So be it. Joyliffe shook his head, as he turned to the left he spotted the stack of fencing foils leaning against the wall near the far corner. There seemed to be a limb sticking out from behind the foils. Could Perkney be hiding there? Foolish man—hide from his sins he could not. Hide from the eye of God? Yea, even in the belly of the whale did not the Lord spy out the sins of Jonah? And he, Jacob Joyliffe, servant of the Lord, was only come to offer Redemption to this sinner. He felt a moment's pang that he had failed to make clear his mission, that was a sorry fault of his own. He'd been swept away by a spate of angry words. He'd answered in kind. Yet his mission was to reason with the man, not to argue with him.

Joyliffe tiptoed over to the corner. A trifle near-sighted, he peered at the stack of foils. Yes, that was a slippered stocking and a well-formed leg sticking out beyond the stack.

"Ah, Perkney, no need to be afraid. I've come to apologize for my hasty words. It was very wrong of me to lose my temper and I hope you will forgive me." He twisted his upper body around the foils, thin brows raised in questioning. The man appeared to be sitting in the corner. Peculiar place to hide, Joyliffe thought. Nor did the dancing master scramble to his feet upon his discovery. Joyliffe stepped around the foils.

"Perkney?" Joyliffe screwed up his eyes in an attempt to penetrate the gloom. He leaned forward. A sudden buzzing filled his head. His heart thudded like the pounding of a galloping horse. Francis Perkney lay slumped against the corner wall, eyes wide and unseeing, jaw dropped in a silent scream, hands clutching at the foil sticking out of his abdomen. Perkney was pinned to the wall like a butterfly in an insect collection.

Joyliffe grabbed the pommel of the sword and pulled. The foil slid out like a knife in butter. Joyliffe fell back a step in surprise. A great gob of black oozed out of the spot where the foil had penetrated. Joyliffe gazed in horror, unable to turn his head from the sight, unable to move, unable to cry out. His brain was filled with wool, his jaw as frozen as the dead man's. His throat was as parched as desert sand. He wanted to cry out above all things, to call for help, to move legs as stiff as Lot who had turned into a pillar of salt. Harvard Divinity hadn't prepared him for this.

Time was suspended. He could not move. How long he stood there he did not know. Only when the cries penetrated his brain and strong arms pinioned him was the spell broken.

"Ho. Help. Murder!"

Yes, yes, he thought with fervent gratitude, that's it. Thank you, he prayed in silence to the unknown shouter. Ho—Help— Murder. That's just what his soul longed to cry out, that his poor physical body refused to utter.

"Ho. Help. Murder!" He stuttered the words all the way to the jail.

ONE

How times have changed. Here am I, Hetty Henry, a mere woman, invited to join in conference with the esteemed young Boston minister, Cotton Mather, and his younger cousin—also a colleague in the ministry—Mister Increase Cotton. All the Mather and Cotton men were in the ministry, so far as I knew. Cotton Mather was the fruit and fruition of the two family branches.

In prior years I'd had to barge my way in on such conferences. I was related to Cotton Mather by his marriage to my cousin Abigail, but I'm much afraid that Cousin Cotton thinks me a forward female. However, I've proved useful to him on several occasions when his ill health prevented him from serving the community and he was expected to get involved.

Creasy, that is Increase Cotton, knows how to ferret out the guilty secrets of the human soul, this from his Harvard College divinity training. I have the connections and the fortune, through my two late husbands, to buy information. We make an efficient team, Creasy and I, when it comes to the delicate matter of murder.

Cousin Cotton Mather is of a sensitive nature, you understand. He suffers from frequent attacks of nerves, especially when called upon to solve a dreadful problem, and murder is certainly that. The fruit of two honored family trees bruises easily. That's where Creasy and I come in. We do his dirty work for him. Creasy is more or less duped into doing it because he feels sorry for his cousin. Creasy and Cotton Mather are first cousins by blood. I do it because it is my duty. And because it relieves my cousin Abigail of much distress.

The matter upon which we were to be consulted was the death of a dancing master, one Francis Perkney, and the arrest of a young Reformed minister for the murder. For myself, I found it difficult to imagine Jacob Joyliffe pinching anyone with a pickle fork, much less slicing the dancing master through with a sword. I'd found Joyliffe a pompous prig, given to fawning over both Cotton Mather and his father, Increase Mather. To some extent I could understand fawning over Uncle Increase, who is a great man here in our Massachusetts Bay colony: diplomat, minister and political power. Increase Mather had negotiated a new charter for the colony with two London monarchs, is head of the largest congregation in the entire New World, and is also President of Harvard College. I held my uncle in great esteem. But you'd think Cotton Mather was a medieval knight in shining armor, mounted on a snow-white steed to boot, the way Joyliffe toadied up to him. Cotton Mather was a bare thirty years to Joyliffe's twenty. I suppose a decade's difference is ancient to a young man. I'm glad I'm not quite that old.

Cousin Cotton appeared to be in ill humor, rather than ill health. His face was flushed and his handsome mouth was puffed out like a flounder. His large eyes were dark with liquid mist which threatened to spill over. My friend Creasy sat sprawled in his chair, his eyes burning like dark coals. It was evident I had walked into a quarrel.

I looked at the two men. "Where's Abigail?" I asked, breaking a strained silence. Abigail is my dearest cousin, with her sweet nature and somewhat dim understanding. Abigail thinks the sun rises and sets for the pleasure of her husband.

Cousin Cotton turned his head to acknowledge my presence. "Murder is not a proper subject for the tender ears of a fair female." His eyes widened as he noted to whom he spoke. Cousin Cotton jumped up from his chair, waving his shapely hand to indicate I should occupy the vacated vessel. "Do forgive me,

Cousin Hetty. I forget my manners." He strode to his desk, slid around it and took his seat there. "This business has me so upset I cannot think straight."

I walked over to take the seat. Cousin Cotton's head followed me like a tufted owl.

"My dear consort will join us with some India tea in a few moments," he said. "No doubt its medicinal properties will soothe our melancholic humors." He glanced at Creasy, who was slouched in his chair, his long legs sprawled across the floor.

"I take it we are here to discover who murdered the dancing master?" I looked from one to the other. Creasy had that stubborn set to his thin lips.

"We know who is the murderer, Cousin Hetty. It's more a matter of preventing the Mather name from being dragged though the mud by this vile creature…this viper…this toad…" In his outburst he jerked his Mather head and the full periwig he wore slid askew. He raised both shapely hands to adjust it. "And the good name of all the ministers in Christ of Boston must be protected, as well. We are all implicated in this disgrace. Do you know what that monster did?" The reddened cheeks grew mottled with pale spots.

Before I could inquire Cousin Cotton rushed on. "He had the effrontery to drop a pamphlet by the body. My father's pamphlet. By the body." Flecks of foam gathered at the corner of his mouth. "My father's famed pamphlet, 'An Arrow against Profane and Promiscuous Dancing,' found next to the body. Now the Mather name is connected to a foul murder. The good Mather name, brought to these shores by my grandfather, the great Richard Mather and illuminated, if I may say so, by my own father, Increase Mather, of Second Church. How dare Perkney destroy our good name with his jealousy, the lowly worm. The viper we nourished in our bosoms… Oh, the words of his mouth were as smooth as butter, yet war was in his heart." He threw his hand, with its long, slender fingers, over his heart, covering a crisp white band upon a brass-buttoned waistcoat of hunter green.

I held up my own hand. "Calm yourself, Cousin." I looked over at my companion in solving crimes, who remained silent in his stubbornness. "Creasy?" I prompted.

"I don't believe Jacob Joyliffe murdered the man." Creasy scowled. He remained sprawled in his seat. At my raised brows he went on, "Just because he found the body, doesn't mean he did the deed. Jacob Joyliffe is innocent of murder. He said he argued with Perkney, not that he killed him. Intemperate words—that's what he said they had. *Intemperate words.*" Creasy emphasized the latter.

"Yes, well to stab a man to death is intemperate, dear cousin, and to leave a copy of 'An Arrow against Profane and Promiscuous Dancing Drawn from the Quiver of the Ministers of Christ at Boston' next to the body to justify that act is calumny and libel." Cotton Mather jabbed a finger in the air.

Creasy pushed back his shoulders against the chair. His longs legs slid forward another inch. "Joyliffe says he returned to Perkney's rooms to apologize. He was so upset upon finding the body he lost all coherence. Poor Joyliffe was in shock, Cousin."

"Oh, of course. Poor Joyliffe. Standing there with a bloody sword in his hand means nothing, I suppose." Cotton Mather threw a glance of angry triumph at his cousin.

"It means Joyliffe tried to help the man by pulling the obscene thing out of the man's guts… I daresay I should have done the same," Creasy said. "It was a natural reaction."

"Call it an unnatural act, rather." Mather leaned over the desk, hands spread atop the polished surface. "Did he cry out? Did he call for help? Did he run for the constable? I am told on excellent authority that he did none of these things. He stood there with the bloody implement in his hands, his victim's blood dripping all over the floor, and he made no move until he was arrested and dragged from the scene of his foul deed. I was told this by none other than Constable Phillymort." Mather sank back into his seat, with a glance of challenge for Creasy.

"That fool Phillymort." Creasy made a face. "Phillymort

would arrest his own mother if she baked a pie on the Sabbath."

I felt I should intervene, as a disinterested party. All Boston talked of the death of the dancing master, but I'd been enmeshed in mercantile affairs. Not until I received the note from Cousin Cotton Mather bidding me to his home had I discussed the murder with anyone.

I addressed myself to the gentleman at the desk. "I trust you have no objection to our making a few discreet inquiries, Cousin Cotton? After all, if we, Creasy and I, discover that someone else had a reason for killing the dancing master, it would help clear the Mather name of any involvement. Not that I think the Mather name is tarnished in any way... Why, how could it be? My dear cousin, I know you to be of such a sensitive nature that this matter causes you great grief. I applaud your efforts to keep the name of your forefathers free of blemish and I assure you, your cousin Creasy and I shall do our outmost to assist you in that endeavor." My face and voice were filled with sympathy, flattery is the best medicine for Cousin Cotton's feelings.

"Ah, Hetty. How sweet is the understanding of woman's mind," Mather groaned. "You do know my upset, my sensitive nature, where the family name is concerned."

I nodded, keeping my expression serious with an effort. Creasy made a face at me.

"There are evil-minded people in this town who would be only too happy to stomp the Mather name in the mud. Great men have enemies, Cousin, and while I am only a tiny gnat, my father is a giant among men. My little abilities are as a seedling beneath the shade of a mighty oak. Such is Increase Mather of Boston. His good name must be protected, Cousin Hetty. Oh, throw me into that mud and let mine enemies trample me, dear Cousin, I care not. Only save my father's good name, I beseech you." He clasped his hands together in prayer.

How could I deny this appeal? A return of Mather's bouts of nerves would mean a dreadful time for my gentle cousin Abigail. His fits of weeping prostrate in the dust upset Abigail no end, especially since my cousin kept her home as neat and ordered as a Sunday sermon. There was not a speck of dust to be found there. She would have to send out for some. Rather than put the sweet soul through such an ordeal, I acquiesced.

I rose from my seat and crossed the room, holding out my hand in fealty. Cotton Mather grasped it as if he were sinking in quicksand. "Cousin Cotton, you may rely upon me, and upon your cousin Creasy, as you well know in your heart. After all, he is named for your illustrious father. Come, Creasy." I turned to him. "Let's go to good Mister Willard, I understand the accused is under house arrest there?"

"That is all he is at the moment, the accused." Creasy shot a stern look at Cotton Mather.

Mather ignored him, with a Saintly smile for me. "Yes, Hetty, do you go and accost the miscreant. I knew I could count upon you to uphold the family honor." This was a parting shot at Creasy, as that gentleman well knew.

I grabbed Creasy's arm and hauled him out of the room.

Two

It proved a difficult task to question the Accused. Jacob Joyliffe appeared to be in a state of shock. A night in the Boston jail certainly hadn't helped him regain his composure. A dirty cell with chains around his ankles, sleeping on urine-soaked straw, is not conducive to dignity. Mister Willard of First Church, that good man, had arranged for Joyliffe's house arrest under his pledge.

Jacob Joyliffe turned his face away at the sight of a woman.

"It's a shame to him," Creasy said to me in a whisper. "Perhaps I should be the one to question him."

I nodded.

"Jacob." Creasy laid a gentle hand upon the prisoner's shoulder. "You know me—it's Creasy Cotton."

"Woe…woe… All is woe," Joyliffe said.

"I have brought my friend, Mrs. Henry, with me, Jacob. We believe in your innocence and we will do our best to obtain justice for you and for the poor unfortunate dancing master."

"Man is wicked," Joyliffe said. His pale blue eyes stared beyond Creasy.

"Man is capable of redemption, Jacob. We will do our best to bring the murderer of the dancing master to that state." Creasy spoke in a gentle tone, as if to a child.

"Man that is born of woman is full of woe," Joyliffe said, ignoring Creasy's words.

"We need your help. Mistress Henry and I would like to ask you a few questions."

"All is woe."

"Can you tell us what happened that day?" Creasy went on, speaking as if Joyliffe understood every word said to him.

"Man is wicked."

"Yes, you were witness to a wicked act, Jacob. There is no doubt about that, and I am very sorry for your distress. Mistress Henry and I are determined to find the man who perpetrated such a wicked act. Can you help us to find this man?"

"Jezebel," Joyliffe said. "Haughty daughters of Zion."

"Is he referring to me?" I turned to Creasy, not altogether pleased. I clenched my fists.

"He doesn't know what he's saying, I'm afraid." Creasy patted the man's shoulder. "Poor fellow."

I wondered if he felt empathy for a fellow minister who was about his own age. Perhaps that empathy would cloud his judgment. I didn't like to agree with Cotton Mather, but what if the young minister was the murderer? Provoked by harsh words, perhaps he had grabbed a foil and run through the dancing master. I determined to remain impartial. So long as the fellow did not call me any more names. Haughty daughter of Zion... As if I went around with jewels in my nose and bells jangling around my ankles. The gentleman's staring into the distance unnerved me. Did he even recognize his visitors? I was ready to take my leave.

"We shan't get anywhere with him," I whispered to Creasy, who argued patience. I had little to spare. There were my mercantile interests to attend and my farm in Rumney Marsh. I'd inherited business properties from my two late husbands and it pleased me to take the management of them upon my own shoulders. I did not run them with such success by suffering fools.

Not that I mean Joyliffe is a fool when he is in his normal mind, but it was quite clear he was not of a normal mind. I felt sorry for the man, but there seemed little sense in waiting for him to attain his usual state, and so I said as much to my companion. Creasy gave me a glance as if I was a heartless wretch but he accepted the arm that I offered and we set off for the scene of the murder.

We went from one fool to another, I thought, as we approached the old warehouse that was the site of the dancing master's rooms. There stood Constable Phillymort with his gold-knobbed staff of office barring our way. Phillymort is an efficient officer of the courts, in his own way, but a more pompous, pious, self-righteous prig does not exist in all of New England. I could tolerate the man in small doses, but my companion loathed the constable. Possibly because he bullied Creasy's congregation of poor souls, chiding them and hauling them into court at the slightest provocation. To be fair, I'd seen the man treat our most honored men of the town in the same manner.

"This place is closed to the public." Phillymort tilted his great staff, barring us from the door. "'What wickedness is this that is done among you?' Judges, Twenty: verse twelve," he quoted.

Creasy's thin black brows knit into a frown, his face turned crimson.

"We are not the public. We are here to investigate the murder of one Francis Perkney, of these premises."

"By whose authority come ye here?" Phillymort's long lower lip thrust out. "'A true witness delivereth souls, but a deceitful witness speaketh lies.' Proverbs Fourteen: verse twenty-five."

"By the authority of a minister of Christ at Boston." Creasy spoke in a frosty tone. He stood as stiff as the constable's staff.

"It is a minister of Christ at Boston who stands accused of the crime. 'The wicked is driven away in his wickedness.' Ibid thirty-two," Phillymort said.

I thought a saw a gleam of satisfaction in the dark eyes beneath the constable's drooping lids. I stifled a smile seeing Creasy ball up his fists.

"Mister Mather sent us." I spoke up, digging my nails into the coat sleeve of my companion. "Cousin Cotton Mather has asked us to come here, on his behalf. You know how busy Mister

Mather is with his church duties and his many interests. I'm sure you wouldn't want to inconvenience him by insisting upon his presence here, although you may feel free to send to him for confirmation of the task he has set us." I flashed my most charming smile at the man, well knowing that the Mathers had appointed him to his job. "Cousin Cotton has asked us to look into the matter of the dancing master's death. He is most concerned for the good name of Mather. We are here to uphold that precious name, I'm sure you understand."

I had uttered the ultimate authority, the name of Mather. The staff of the constable was lowered, although the body of the constable still blocked the way. I batted my golden eyelashes at the man. "Will you not assist us, Sir, by escorting us to the fateful spot? I should be less fearful for my safety with Constable Phillymort by my side."

While these womanly tactics have proven useful in the past, the Constable lacked the instincts of a true gentleman. He ignored me, his gaze passing over my head to focus upon my companion.

"'A continual dropping in a very rainy day and a contentious woman are alike.' Proverbs twenty-seven, twelve," the constable intoned.

We were allowed to pass—that is, Creasy dragged me inside before I could kick the constable in his skinny shin.

Before the door slammed, leaving us in near darkness, I caught a glimpse of a long room. We stopped, waiting for our eyes to adjust to the gloom. The musty smell of an empty warehouse depressed the chilly air. Beside me I heard Creasy shifting his feet.

"I can't see," he whispered. "Let me go outside and make the constable hold open the door until we find a candle."

I pressed his arm, warning him not to move. "Shhh. I hear something." I strained to listen. It might be no more than a mouse. Or a murderer. There it was again, a faint scritch-scratch sound. Not a mouse, a rat maybe. 'A rat behind the arras.' The quote came unbidden to my mind and I shivered. Hamlet had stabbed the rat behind the arras. Someone had stabbed the dancing master to death.

Creasy swung his arm in front of me, forcing me back a step. "Is anyone here?" His words rang out in the echoing space. Yes, the ghost of Hamlet's father, I thought to myself. I half expected the King of Denmark to materialize out of the gloom. The hair on the back of my neck prickled.

A light floated towards us from the far darkness, yet I could see no human face behind it. The light shimmered like a will-o-wisp, but this was not a swamp nor was it a hot summer's eve when such sights are seen. It was a dreary March afternoon in Boston with piles of snow on the shady sides of the streets and wet mud on the sides where the sun filtered through the clouds. I stood speechless, my brain as frozen as my body. I did not think to cry out for help, although the constable stood just beyond the door.

With his arm out to protect me, Creasy called in his best sermonizing voice, loud and stern, "Identify yourself. This is a minister of Christ who addresses you."

I wondered if announcing oneself as a minister was such a good idea. How would it affect the spirit? If this were the ghost of the dancing master, would it not take revenge upon a colleague of the minister accused of murdering him? Would he understand that Creasy was only a colleague and not his murderer? Does a ghost recognize his killer enough to differentiate? I hoped the dancing master's spirit was half as intelligent as Hamlet's father. Perhaps he could give us the details of his murder, as did the King of Denmark. Perhaps we ought to reassure it that we came to bring it justice. 'Avenge thy father's spirit...' Well, we were not here to avenge, but perhaps we could bring it peace under the law. I grabbed Creasy's arm and hung on.

I hope I am no coward but the apparition that appeared before my eyes was horrid, as if it had pushed its way up from the mud of the grave. Two ghastly eyes and a gaping maw in a white shroud peered behind the light. I would have shrieked but my mouth froze.

Creasy dropped his arm, my only shield, and I stumbled against him.

"Mister Henry," he said. "Why didn't you say who you were? You gave me a start."

Mister Henry… The ghost of my late husband? I hung on to Creasy for dear life. What had I done to drive him from the grave? How could I appease him? My transgressions were many, I knew, but most of them took place long after my late husband's burial. I had truly mourned him. I hope I honored him by seeking justice, as would he, in his position as a magistrate. I knew it was every citizen's duty to keep the laws of the community. Creasy and I had unearthed, no, that was the wrong choice of words: we worked together to uncover the guilty secrets of the murderer. We had some successes at it, enough so that we had been called in to find the murderer of Francis Perkney, the dancing master. So why has he c-come for me? I stammered, but my words refused to form into coherent speech.

THREE

I gave my head a shake. My Mister Henry? I forced myself to take a closer look as the apparition lowered its candle. A dark complexioned face with unseeing eyes stared back at me.

"This is Henry, Perkney's servant." Creasy shook off my hands, which were clenched upon the cloth of his coat. "No need to be afraid, Hetty. He's a member of my church. I know him very well."

Henry held a dark finger up to his mouth, signifying silence. He beckoned us with his free hand, leading us forward with the candle held in its black holder before him. We followed to the end of a hallway, where the servant stopped and turned to face us.

The servant's eyes were a blue-mottled white but the mouth flashed white teeth and the shroud was nothing but a white shirt and a small powered wig. When he spoke it was in a low, melodic voice.

"I am not supposed to be in here, Mister Cotton," he said. "Constable Phillymort would not allow it. I came to get my fiddle, Sir, and my good coat, which I wear when I play for Master Perkney. How am I to make a living without my fiddle? Who will hire a blind servant? I tried to explain that to the constable but he wouldn't listen. I came in through the back way."

"There's a back way?" Creasy seemed surprised.

"It's hard to find. Master Francis didn't want people to know about it—only certain persons."

"You'd better show us, Henry. Oh, this is Mrs. Henry. I mean Mrs. Hetty Henry," he amended.

"You may call me Hetty," I said, in haste.

"Well, Missus, I didn't think you was my wife." The servant flashed his teeth in a good-humored grin.

"Hetty is helping me look into the murder of Mr. Perkney," Creasy explained.

"But, Constable Phillymort said they caught the murderer." Henry turned, held the candle up for us to see and led us to a doorway.

"I don't agree with the constable." Creasy's voice grew hard. "I don't believe Mr. Joyliffe killed the man. I don't believe he could kill anyone."

"I am glad to hear it, Sir," Henry said. "I did not like to think a minister of God could do such a thing."

Creasy nodded, as if the blind man could see him. "Perhaps you can help us, Henry."

The skepticism I felt must have been apparent. A blind man? He could have been in the same room, stood beside the man and not have known who murdered the dancing master.

"Henry has his wits about him, Hetty." Creasy rebuked me with his tone. "He knows more about Francis Perkney than anyone else."

"I served Master Francis for seven years. He was always good to me, and to my wife." Henry spoke as he sought and found the latch. "This is his private apartment."

He opened the door with a minimum of fumbling, I noted. We entered a fair sized room, dominated by a large bed hung with green velvet curtains and golden, knotted pulls. The curtains were closed. The only window in the room was high up and emitted little light. Henry went around the room with unerring precision, lighting candles in the wall sconces from his own candle. Beneath the window the new light revealed a small table, two straight-backed wooden chairs and a desk. There was a chest of drawers against the wall opposite to the bed and next to it stood a table with a pitcher and washbasin upon it. A dark wooden rack held hand cloths. A large chest stood at the foot of the bed. Very much the establishment of a bachelor. Except for the bed. I wandered over and fingered the soft velvet.

"May I draw back the bed curtains?" I asked of Henry. I was curious, the rest of the room was Spartan, but the dancing master had not stinted in the bed. What were the linens like? I drew back the curtain and gasped with delight at the carved posts of glistening dark wood. They spiraled in graceful curves up to a simple finial. The pillows and sheets were fresh and crisp, the linen edged with soft lace. The coverlet was tapestry in muted shades of green and gold.

"It's beautiful, this bed." I said for Henry's benefit.

"My wife collects and washes the linens once a week." Henry spoke with pride. "I make up the bed every morning, myself. Master Francis wanted it just so. We have two dozen sheets."

"Who will inherit?" I asked. Inheritance might be a motive for murder, after all. I might even be tempted to kill for a bed like this. I amended my thoughts with haste, asking the Lord to forgive my greed. Still, it was a valid question.

Henry, however, did not have the answer. "I don't know as Master Perkney had any kith or kin."

No fire had been lit for days and the old building seeped damp and cold. I looked once more with longing upon the inviting warmth of the tapestry coverlet, pulled my cloak tight about me, and drew closed the hangings.

Henry led us around the bed to a small alcove. "Master Francis kept his bottles of wine here. He didn't keep no food—he went to the tavern to eat his meals." Henry picked up a leather fire bucket and set it back on the floor. "There are some fire buckets and a broom." He set the candlestick with care upon a shelf. The flame flared and receded. There was no other light in the alcove. He pushed at the back wall and a small door opened. It led outside into a stack of firewood, or so I thought until I saw a path between the cords.

"The door can be barred from the inside but not from outside. Most of the time Master Francis left the door unbarred.

Only when he was entertaining the ladies…" Henry stopped. His milk-clouded eyes stared into the wood stack.

Creasy glanced at me. "Don't worry about Hetty, Henry— I mean Hetty is a lady, there is no doubt about that, but she knows the world. You may speak frankly in front of her. Mayn't he, Hetty?"

"You may, Henry," I said. "Come, let us go back inside and you tell us about those ladies. It might well have a bearing on the murder. Don't be shy about telling us the truth."

Henry nodded. I backed into the alcove and picked up the candle, holding it so I could better see what was on the shelves. There lay a row of bottles, as Henry had said, with three tall, green-stemmed goblets that were quite handsome, four pewter mugs, two leather flasks and an open box of candles. The floor held the fire buckets, a broom and several cracked chamber pots.

We entered the bedchamber, filed past the bed and stepped over to the table. Henry pulled out a chair so that I could seat myself. Creasy took the other chair. Henry remained standing. "Didn't I see a stool in the big room as we came through, Henry? Why don't you retrieve it and join us."

Henry preferred to stand. The stool, he said, was where he sat to play the fiddle for the dancing. I asked him about the dancing.

"Yes, how many came here?" Creasy asked.

"Oh, sometimes we could get up a dozen sets," Henry said. "Them was lively times. But most it was the ladies come for a lesson by themselves."

"Then he brought them in here for a little tête-à-tête." I pursed my mouth and glanced at Creasy. The servant misunderstood me, however.

"I don't know about no tattletales, Ma'am." Henry shook his head. "I ain't no tattletale. I kept quiet. Master Francis wanted it that way."

Creasy frowned at me, a warning to keep my own silence.

"Master Perkney is dead, Henry. You may speak freely about his lady friends. Hetty and I will keep your confidence as much as the law permits. But it is necessary that we know the names of those ladies. By telling us, you may help us catch his murderer. His death releases you of any vows to the man."

"If you say so, Mister Cotton, Sir." Henry stared ahead with his blind eyes.

"I do say so." Creasy spoke in a gentle voice. "Now, what are the names of those ladies who came for dancing lessons?"

I was a bit skeptical about this question. How would Henry know anything about those ladies? He couldn't describe their features or their dress, which would have told me much. And they might well have used false names to come here. The ministers were on a crusade against any kind of court dances. They could not keep people from dancing the old country dances, though, in spite of the minister's disapproval for any form of dance between man and woman.

"I know them, Mister Cotton. Oh, not because Master Francis told me anything about them. Master Francis was always the gentleman. But I played the fiddle for them, you see, and got to know their names and the way they talked—especially how they laughed. Master Francis would tell me that he had an appointment at ten o'clock or eleven o'clock with Mrs. Carp or at noon with Mrs. Ellicott and I must play only country dances for her, otherwise her husband would not let her come. Then there was Mrs. Welsteed. My master was very taken with her, I could tell. And Mrs. Binning, I think she is a widow lady. Master Francis was very particular in his attentions to her."

I nearly fainted at these names. I knew all of them. Caroline Carp, the meek little lady with the frightened eyes and her tall, gloom-faced husband, the major, Mary Ellicott the high and mighty, far too proper for the likes of Hetty Henry, although I could buy out her husband's warehouse twelve times over. Sarah Welsteed—well, that was a surprise. I thought Sarah quite happy in her marriage, although the captain was often away at sea. Betsy Binning, the widow, I could understand. I was twice widowed and vowed never to marry again, so I could not blame Betsy for taking her happiness where she could. My thoughts were interrupted by Henry's further recital of two more names. These two ladies were English chapel. That is, they belonged to the Church of England, so I did not know them very well. However my hand flew to my bosom at the capacity of the dancing master.

"Wait, Henry," I said. "These are all women who took dancing lessons or women who went to his bed?"

"Both, Ma'am."

My admiration for the late Mister Perkney increased. Clearly I had neglected my education. I should have found the time for dancing instruction.

As for my companion, Creasy's thin black brows had disappeared into his hairline. His mouth hung open. I knew that the man was no prude. Creasy was very gallant, if more than a little naïve, when it came to women. The numbers of names brought out the Reformed church within him. I gathered he was thinking of the hours he must spend, kneeling beside these women in prayer so that he might bring them to Redemption. His ministerial duties weighted heavily upon him, I'm sure. I was thinking of the angry husbands who had reason for murder. We had no shortage of suspects here. One could not eliminate the women, either. If one found out about the others, Master Perkney was bound for a bad end.

"But Henry," I managed to stammer, "how do you know, well, that ladies were in this bedchamber?" The man was blind, after all.

"Oh, Ma'am, I would hear them laugh through the wall sometimes, and I could smell them when I made the bed of a morning."

He seemed to have guessed my wonderment that a blind man could tell one woman from another. "Mrs. Binning," he went on, "now, that lady has a smell of lavender about her, very nice and sweet, and she spoke often to me when I played for her. She gave me a shilling every week. I'd know her light step, even if I could not see her. And Mrs. Ellicott has a smell of the ocean..."

Yes, of dead fish and wet seaweed.

"Mrs. Ellicott has a high laugh that hurt my ears, but I only heard her laugh when she was in this room with my master. Mrs. Carp, now, has a low, quiet laugh and a smell like Hispaniola, when I was a boy, before I was sold and brought to this country. She is like the wild flowers there," he said in explanation. "And Mrs. Welsteed. She has a laugh like sleigh bells. She always smells like the wild roses on the beach. I can tell one woman from another, even though I am blind, Ma'am. Everyone has a step or sound or a smell, man or woman, and it's easy to know if you must."

I wondered what aroma I wafted in my wake. As if he read my thoughts, the blind man spoke in answer. "Salt and apple blossoms. You smell like springtime, Mrs. Henry. And I'd know Mr. Cotton anywhere by his step. He walks forward, light on his feet, and he carries the smell of ink and old paper and wood smoke about him."

I wrinkled my nose and sniffed. "Why, he does." I turned to Creasy. "You smell of old books, Creasy."

"You see, Mrs. Henry, I am blind but I can see in my own way." Henry's voice held a gentle rebuke.

"I believe you, Henry," I said. He had convinced me with his remarkable powers of observation.

"And I think there were men in here, too." Henry spoke in a solemn tone.

At our collective gasps Henry went on. "I don't mean in the bed, I mean in this room. Sometimes when I came in of a morning there was the smell of tobacco and leather or rum and fish. My master did not smoke a pipe, nor does he drink rum, although he has a flask of it in the alcove. But my master chose not to tell me about them and I never heard them talk or laugh, so I don't know who they were." Henry paused, waiting for more questions.

Creasy obliged. "Didn't Mister Perkney give fencing lessons as well as dance instruction?"

Henry nodded, and Creasy went on. "Perhaps he invited them in for a mug of rum after a lesson. That would be an agreeable thing to do." He leaned forward, hands upon his long knees, and pushed himself up from the chair. "You've been most help-ful, Henry."

I took my cue from Creasy and rose as well.

"May I take my violin and my best coat now, Mister Cotton?"

"You may, Henry, and good luck to you. You know you may come to me if you need assistance. You, or your wife."

"One more question, Henry, before you leave." I slipped a coin into the dark fist. "Did Mister Perkney keep a diary or a ledger? If so, where are they to be found?"

"Oh, I do know that he kept his accounts in a big book. He wrote in that book every evening. Before I left for the night I sharpened a quill and set out the pot of ink on this very table. I can't say as what he wrote in it. I can't read, even had I the sight. He keeps—kept it there, in that chest." He pointed to the kingly bed. "I knew by the sound of the hinge creak."

We left the bedroom together and returned to the large room where the dancing lessons were taught. Henry picked up a parcel behind the stool and slipped back to the bedchamber to make his exit through the hidden door.

We did not hear him leave. Creasy and I stood before the stack of fencing foils, raising our candles and taking in the dull stains upon the wooden floor where the dead man had lain.

FOUR

"Do you think it could have been an accident?" I kept my voice low. Even with the wall sconces ablaze the spot seemed desolate. "A fencing lesson gone wrong? Perhaps the perpetrator went into a panic and ran away."

Creasy shook his head. "I don't think so. From what I've heard, Mister Perkney wasn't wearing a mask or chest protection. Surely he wouldn't have taught a lesson without a mask. We'll have to ask the man who found Joyliffe standing over the body. Phillymort will know who it was."

"Yes, well... I'll leave the pleasure of speaking to the constable to you. I will speak to the women involved with Mister Perkney—you talk to the men." Cousin Cotton Mather was correct in one thing, this is a delicate matter. "You'll have to find out where the husbands were at the time," I continued. "You must take care not to betray the wives. You won't tell the husbands..." My voice dropped off. I felt anxious on this point. It was certainly Creasy's duty as a Reformed minister to bring the sinners to repentance, but I counted upon the tolerance he'd shown in the past. Creasy was particularly susceptible to the ladies, therefore I would have to question them.

Creasy frowned down at me. "Not even Cousin Cotton would betray their trust. He'd pray with them in private and not reveal their names or sins to anyone, as shall I. It's our duty to bring people to Redemption through their own will, not to coerce them. We've seen enough of that in Salem."

At the mention of Salem I shivered. So many souls lost, and a near thing I wasn't one of them. It was Uncle Increase Mather, Cotton's father, who finally put a stop to that madness. He gathered the ministers of Boston in a published protest called "Cases of Conscience." He'd also put pressure upon Governor Phipps. Of course, the governor wasn't too happy with the Salem judges when his own wife was accused of being a witch. And all the time Cousin Cotton lay cowering in the nonexistent dust of his room, in the throes of melancholia. I have noticed that these bouts occur whenever a crisis occurs and he is called upon to solve it. Poor Abigail, my own sweet cousin, is driven to distraction with the work and the worry of caring for the invalid. For her sake alone I would be driven to assist in righting the community, did I not feel it my duty as a citizen to help.

"What shall we do about the Church of England ladies?" I asked, turning to my companion. "Their names are not familiar to me. I don't know that they would even receive me, much less confide in me. Yet I hate to think of having Phillymort question them. Even Church of England members do not deserve such treatment."

Creasy agreed with a stiff laugh. "No doubt they would be treated as Whores of Babylon and thrown into prison, causing a great deal of consternation from our friends of that faith. Perhaps M'sieur Germaine would help us." Creasy paused to consider the matter.

M'sieur Germaine is a Huguenot merchant, a refugee from France, with ties to the English chapel merchants. Creasy is very impressed with the gentleman, who is most genial, to be fair to him. M'sieur likes to give dinners and dances. I thought for a moment. We could certainly wangle an invitation to M'sieur's next dinner. A word in the French gentleman's ear and we could arrange to be seated next to the two English chapel ladies with an opportunity to gossip with them. The death of the dancing master was bound to be the chief topic of the evening's conversation. Once we'd been introduced I was certain we could discover their whereabouts on the afternoon of the murder.

"Yes," I spoke in a decided tone. "Yes. If you will please ask
M'sieur for a place at his table, I would be much obliged." I related my seating plan. "Perhaps we'll have a chance to speak to
the husbands, too. You'll be able to confirm what they tell you
easily enough." For a minister of the Reformed Church, Creasy
had the knack for making friends with the Church of England
members. He felt easier in their company than I did, and I knew
many of the men from commerce. He could overlook theological differences—well, so I could I for that matter—but I could
not forget a long history of persecution of our churches. Even in
this new world, the former Royal Governor, the Tyrant, Andros,
had arrested ministers, confiscated Mister Willard's church for
his services and left the elderly and frail to stand out in the rain.
On the other hand, M'sieur Germaine gave very tasty dinners. I
held nothing against the French Protestants.

Creasy lowered his candle. "Let's go back into the other room.
We might as well get started looking through Perkney's possessions. I don't like this part of it, Hetty. Prying into a victim's per-
sonal possessions…it doesn't seem right."

Creasy looked to me as if for reassurance, which I was quite
ready to give. "It must be done," I said. I was curious to discover
what secret drew so many women to the dancing master.

"Letters." Creasy's thin brows twisted into a knot of disapproval. "There have to be letters. Poor deluded creatures." He
shook his head in sympathy for the weakness of women.

"So many of them," I said, smiling inwardly. The women's fol-
lies were safe with him. I need not worry he would expose them,
unless absolute necessity drove him to it. One had to respect that
he took his priestly duties seriously. I touched his coat sleeve.

"I can do it," I said. "Go home and rest. You look tired." The
atmosphere in the deserted building was heavy with stale air and
smoke. The fact that a bloody crime had been committed here
added to the depressing weight. "We can do this tomorrow," I
added as an alternative. Perhaps he would not like to leave me

by myself in this building. I did not mind staying by myself, now that I knew the place wasn't haunted by the ghost of the King of Denmark.

I really wanted to get at those boxes and the great chest by the bed, but perhaps my companion's spirits would recover after a good night's rest. Creasy was prone to bouts of self-doubt. Sometimes I wondered if he carried the burden of his relationship to the two Mathers, father and son, whose reputations were known in England as well as in the colonies. Creasy's congregation was mostly poor widows, sailors and laborers, yet I felt his to be the happier lot. I'd never seen Creasy fall upon his knees, weeping and wailing in the dust. It's just that he needed reminding and sometimes a good scold to put him back in humor. I was happy to provide that service.

"We'll come back tomorrow, then," I said. "Let me just get that ledger and bring it home with me. I can examine it tonight and tell you about its contents tomorrow morning. A ledger can reveal many things about the man—or woman, for that matter—who keeps it." I kept my own ledgers, although a clerk entered the day-to-day transactions. I slipped into the private room. Creasy following behind but remaining by the door.

I opened the big chest, my hand holding the heavy cover above my head. I peered around but could not spot anything that resembled a ledger. "Creasy, come over with a candle. I can't see."

The man obliged. I suddenly realized why the cover was so heavy. In a shelf beneath the chest cover a large bound leather book fitted neatly inside. "Here, hold the cover while I take the ledger out," I said. With the weight lifted from my hand I reached in for the book. I had to waggle it to get it part way out.

"Wait," Creasy said. "That's a big book. How will we get it past the constable?"

I considered sneaking it out the back way, but Creasy rebuked me. "You can't do that. We have to go out the front or Phillymort will come in to look for us. Do you want him nosing around in here?"

Most certainly. I didn't want him turning the room upside down in his effort to uncover the dancing master's possessions, and I certainly did not want him to examine this ledger. He would not know how to read it properly nor would he share it with me, even if I ran my late husbands' two mercantile adventures with efficiency and profit. I was a mere woman, after all. With a grimace I shoved the book back into its resting place.

Creasy gave a sigh of relief when I did not argue with him. "We'll leave it until tomorrow. We can do a thorough search in the morning," he said.

I gathered that he did not want to argue with the constable or be the butt of the man's thinly veiled theological insults.

"It is getting late, and I've a mind for some supper. Milk's tavern?" I suggested a favorite spot of ours.

Creasy nodded. He looked relieved. I know the air felt lighter as we passed the constable without speaking to him and walked in the dusk to the tavern. We dodged bodies, carts and horses as people scurried to their homes for their suppers. A feeling of envy touched me for those fortunate enough to return to a warm hearth, a welcome, and a good supper from a comforting presence. I wondered if Creasy felt the same. He'd lost his fiancée a year ago. So far as I knew, he courted no one now. Oh, I'd no mind to marry again, myself—this feeling would evaporate as quickly as it came.

We turned an alley corner, trudging a muddy path. I wore clogs of wood and leather to keep my slippers safe but my toes felt like ice. I pulled my cloak tight about me.

"Creasy, do you ever think of marriage?" I could not help my curiosity.

"Of course I will marry some day, the Lord willing. Why—are you reconsidering my offer?" He stopped, his voice sharp.

Since his offer of marriage was made under duress and since Mister Increase Cotton was the last man on earth that I would consider for marriage, if I were going to consider marriage, my tone was as sharp as his. "No!" I pulled on his arm, forcing him forward. Softening my voice to appease him, I continued. "But you should marry. Wouldn't it be sweet to be greeted by a comely wife with a warm fire in the hearth and a warm supper on the table? I was just remembering those pleasures. There are times when I miss the company of a husband."

"Easily solved, Hetty. There are any number of men who would gladly marry you, and you know it."

I wrinkled my nose. "There are those who would gladly marry me for my wealth. There are many of them. But you know I've no mind to marry again. I lost two good men—it's enough. Besides, I like my life as it is. And we were talking about you."

"When the Lord is willing, I shall find such a companion," he said.

I looked up at Creasy but his face was tranquil. I thought of his dead fiancée. We had argued about her shortly before her death, and I still felt some guilt for that. Well, I could not know she was going to die when I told him she was not the right woman for him. He didn't speak to me for months afterward.

We reached the tavern and ordered a cold meal of Indian pudding, beef and bread, with a mug of cider to wash it down. Creasy broke the silence of our chomping after we'd both taken the edge off our hunger.

"Promise me you won't go back there tonight to get that ledger. You are thinking of it, aren't you?"

I nodded. There was no use telling a lie to this man.

Creasy shook a long finger. "There's a killer on the loose, Hetty. He could be hiding in there. Promise me you won't go without me."

"What makes you so sure it's a man?" I hoped to distract my companion as I challenged him. "A woman could have done it just as easily. Perhaps even more so. He would be on his guard with a man, not so with a woman. You men think we are such helpless creatures."

Creasy smiled, a long and loose smile that brightened his somber face. "Not I, not since I've known you, Hetty. I don't think you are a helpless creature at all. It's just that a fencing foil

doesn't seem to be a woman's weapon, that's all. You just promise me you won't go back there tonight."

I gave a grudging promise, since I could not distract him
with argument as I used to. He insisted upon walking me to my
door, which I thought insulting rather than gallant. Clearly he
did not trust me to keep my promise. I keep rooms over my late
husband's warehouse. As I climbed the stairs I knew Creasy stood
outside in the dark, watching lest I sneak out on him. I undressed
and climbed into my bed very aggrieved at his lack of faith, even
if the thought had crossed my mind.

As dawn peeped though the night sky with her rosy glow, I
unbarred my front door. There stood Creasy, rubbing his eyes,
his black hair in a tangled mop.

"What—did you stand out there all night long?" I felt quite
indignant. Lack of trust is one thing, but being fool enough to
keep me under watch the entire night—that smacked of tyran-
ny...or a jealous husband.

"I told you I'd be here first thing, and no, I didn't stand here
all night. I went home and had a full night's sleep. I just had
some problems waking up, that's all, and I thought I'd be late so
I rushed to dress." He ran his hand through the shock of black
hair, attempting to smooth it into some order. He had a black
ribbon falling from the back of his neck.

"If you wore a periwig you wouldn't have that problem," I
said, walking around him to inspect him.

"I don't want to wear a periwig."

"Even Cousin Cotton Mather wears a full periwig."

"Uncle Increase Mather does not."

Creasy's voice was sharp and I could not argue with him this
early in the morning. I am not in my best nature at this time of
day. Besides, I could not berate his sloppy dress when I myself
had thrown on my oldest gown of striped wool and covered it
with an old rust colored cloak. My black hood covered my own
wayward brushing of my hair. There was a decided chill in the
air. "Milk's again?" I suggested.

Milk's Tavern served a fine breakfast for just such a damp,

chilly morning. Platters of chops, pumpkin sauce and warm johnnycake with creamy butter appeared on the table beside a frothy pitcher of cider.

I stripped out of my cloak, revealing my work-a-day clothing. Creasy gave me a critical look but was intelligent enough to say nothing. I noted that he rearranged and tightened the ribbon around his queue in an attempt to control his unruly hair. We both set to work upon the chops with a hearty appetite. When I'd drained the last of my cider, I threw back my head content with the world.

"Let's sneak into Perkney's rooms by the back way," I spoke with a yawn, stretching my arms over my head. "I don't know about you but I can't answer for what I'll do to Constable Phillymort if he insults me this morning."

Creasy munched on a last piece of johnnycake and swallowed. "The sanctimonious prig." He sighed. "No, let's not give him that satisfaction. We have every right to be there. It's our duty to be there. I say we walk right past him…ignore him as if he is not there."

"And if he hits us with that great big staff?" I wondered aloud.

"If he even tries to stop us, you grab one end of the staff, I'll grab the other, and we'll bowl him right over."

I had to laugh at the picture. I stood up, feeling in a far more optimistic mood. "Come on. I want to get a look at that ledger."

As we discovered, the constable was not there to bully us. In his place an old man lay snoring on the steps, curled up as if he were sleeping in the softest down bed. We had to step over him to reach the door. "The watchman needs a watchman," I said.

The morning light did not penetrate into the interior of the dancing school. Creasy found and lit a candle to guide us to the private rooms. I could not help a glance of apprehension as we reached the door, unable to keep my gaze from the site of the murder. All I could make out was a stack of fencing foils. They stood sentinel over the spot like the ghosts of Spanish soldiers, which fancy I did not share with Creasy. I felt an ache in my bowels, although that might be the pumpkin sauce. Was I becoming squeamish in my old age? After all, I was nearly twenty and eight years.

Creasy opened the door. I crowded in behind. I'm not usually such a timid soul but there something dreary about this place. I am used to a warehouse full of goods, bundles and carts, with laborers bustling back and forth. The silence of this empty hall unnerved me.

A shaft of light from the high window shone across the great velvet bed, which sight cheered me. At least this bed had known its share of pleasures. Creasy went around lighting the wall sconces while I scurried over to the chest. I knelt on the floor beside it—that's why I had worn my oldest gown—and lifted the lid. It opened with ease. I reached into the compartment to remove the ledger. My fingers wiggled in open space. I thrust them as far back as they could go, still I did not feel the weight of a bound book. I thrust my head inside the chest, peering into the dark interior. Had I mistaken the compartment? My arms were tiring with the weight of the lid. I leaned over, bumping my head on the lid with a sharp crack.

"Ouch!" I yelled, letting out a curse. I pulled back, the lid dropping from my hands with a dull thud.

"What the devil? What are you doing, Hetty? I nearly jumped out of my skin."

"Creasy, it's gone." I howled with frustration. Even to my own ears I sounded like a wailing child.

Creasy clumped to my side, raising the candle for better light. "What? What's gone?"

"It's gone. The ledger is gone. It's not here. Someone took it, and it's all your fault." I turned upon my companion, taking out my disappointment upon him. I banged upon the lid with my fists. "It's gone. It's gone. Someone has stolen it." There are times when I become somewhat unreasonable, especially when I'm deprived of something I want.

Creasy stood there, candle in hand, rubbing his head with his free fist.

I looked up at him. "I told you we should have snuck back last night, but no… Somebody else got it and we'll never find out who the killer is. Are you satisfied?"

Creasy's hand froze to the top of his head.

"Why do I listen to you? Why. Do. I. Listen. To. You."

Creasy was stung into words. "And maybe you would've come back and been killed by the murderer. Did you ever think of that, Mistress Scold?"

I hate it when he calls me that, especially when he's right to do so. I made myself take three deep breaths.

"Did you ever think the constable might have taken it into his keeping? The ledger is sure to be evidence in the case." Creasy rebuked me with his stiff tone. "He probably came in after we left to see if we'd stolen anything ourselves. You know Phillymort."

I sat back on my heels, a ray of hope rising within my bosom. "Yes. That would be like him, wouldn't it? Sorry," I added. This was as close as I could come as an apology for my childish tantrum.

"We might as well take inventory of the chest. I brought paper and there's pen and ink in that desk." He gestured to the clerk's desk on thin wooden legs. "There's no stool. Master Perkney must have penned his love-missives while standing," Creasy said. "You shout out the contents and I'll write 'em down." He ambled over to the desk.

I glanced over at him, meaning to agree. "Love missives. That's it, Creasy. There have to be love letters. You search the desk while I search the chest. We're bound to come up with something. A man like Perkney keeps his love letters as souvenirs…perhaps even blackmail. Now, that would be a reason for murder, wouldn't it?" I felt my face flush with excitement. Love letters could be more incriminating than a ledger—if we could find them first. Since there was no sign of disarray in the room, the constable must not have searched the place. We hadn't mentioned love letters yesterday. If he'd been listening at the door he might have heard us talk about a ledger, though. It would be just like Phillymort to do such a thing, and to remove the ledger so he'd have it instead of me. I must confront Phillymort about it.

I ducked my head into the open chest and pulled at piles of white shirts, lace collars and sweet smelling linens. The gentleman must have been a fastidious dresser. I wasn't going to count. I waggled my fingers down to the bare wood of the bottom. I felt no paper letters or waxy seals, however. I tried from one side to the other. Letters could be hidden inside cloth, so I removed the shirts one after another, fingering each one for concealed love notes. I could take the time to be thorough, I reasoned.

Creasy hummed as he pulled out packets of paper from cubbies, examined them and thrust them back in. I found his humming annoying but did not want to argue with him over it. I'd been ill tempered enough this morning. My temper was a grievous fault in me, one I'd have to make public confession at Sunday's meeting. Perhaps I'd go to Creasy's church instead of Second Church on Sunday. Uncle Increase took my sins with such a saddened countenance I was quite ashamed of myself on his behalf. So had Cousin Cotton Mather a solemn face, but he was secretly reveling in my confessions so he could offer to pray with me before my cousin Abigail. Abby is such a sweet thing, she would feel pain for me. Then I'd want to inflict real pain on Cousin Cotton and have to restrain myself. A good swift kick in the shins.

I was interrupted in my ruminations by a loud exclamation from Creasy at the desk.

"What is it?" I began to rise from the floor.

"Letters. The letters. Tied with different color ribbons, and there seems to be a different hand writing on each packet." He turned to me, waving a handful of letters. A red ribbon dangled in the air like a streak of blood.

FIVE

We argued about who would examine the contents of the letters Creasy found in the desk. I wasn't about to let him read the things while I sorted out a pile of shirts. I wanted to discover the secret of the late dancing master's seductive allure.

"But Creasy." I slipped a finger to my lips in caution. "There may be passages that are unsuitable for a clergyman's eyes. You might condemn the writer for her immoral behavior, even without meaning to do so. You will lose your objectivity to solving this murder."

Creasy shook his head, swiftly shoving the packet of letters behind his back as if to protect them from my greedy claws.

"These letters were meant to be private, read by one man only," I argued. "Think of the poor women's feelings if they knew a minister of the Lord perused their guilty words. I could censor them for you, and read you the sections relative to motive for the man's murder." I thought this a reasonable offer on my part. Surely it was better if a fellow female's eyes saw the words.

"Oh, I think my eyes have seen enough unsuitable behavior to stand a few passionate phrases, Hetty. You of all people should know that."

"Are you accusing me of unsuitable behavior?" I felt my face grow warm. Creasy treated on dangerous grounds here. I was guilty of such behavior.

He held up his hand, the long fingers spread into a fan. "I only meant that you should know I wouldn't condemn the poor women out of hand. Have I not sins of my own to ponder? Did not the Lord say to *judge not, lest ye be judged?*"

I had to admit the right of his questions. I stood by the chest.

"We'll split the letters. The reading will go quicker that way." Creasy turned and began to pull out packets of letters. "One for you." He tossed me a pile. "One for me. One for you, one for me." He droned on until we had six packets each, all in different colored ribbons.

"Twelve women," I exclaimed at the man's appetite. "But Henry only told us about six. Wait," I added. "Some of these are old." I unfolded a missive and gave it a brief glance. "This is from the New York colony. It's marked from Long Island. I'm going to toss out the yellowing ones. They don't concern us."

"Could not one of the poor cast-offs followed the dancing master to Boston?" Creasy asked. "Is it wise to toss them aside as Perkney seems to have done?"

"Well you read them if you want, although it doesn't seem possible for a married woman to come as far as Boston without notice. And he chose married women or widows for his dalliances." Let Creasy do as he chose. I wouldn't argue with him this time. There was too much fodder in these letters to waste time in disputation with an opinionated minister. Disputation was a hazard of his profession.

"But we'll share the good ones. Agreed?" I prodded with enthusiasm. At his nod I slammed shut the chest lid and sat down upon it with my pile of letters.

Reading other people's letters proved to be a difficult task. First, it was often difficult to decipher the handwriting, second, the misspelling of the words was appalling. Not that I wasn't as guilty in misspelling as some of these women, but correspondence in my merchant ventures taught me to write plain, in simple phrases, and to the point. These letters were expressions of deep passions, private thoughts, and I felt an invader here. I knew these women—or thought I did. Sarah Welsteed's pink-ribboned packet held letters short and light in tone, flirtatious rather than passionate or beseeching. Some were explanations as to why she must forego "the pleasure of his lessons," others set a date and time with no stronger sentiments than "Adieu" above her signature. Reading a lack of deep emotion or attachment in her tone, I didn't think she could be the killer. Well, to tell truth I didn't think she could be the killer anyway. Her nature was too cheerful.

I was eager to read the effusions of Mary Ellicott—she who thought she was so far above me in breeding and birth. I opened the packet, but as I read, I found myself feeling sorry for the woman. Her letters were protestations of great regard for a man whom she charged felt but little regard for her or her situation. *My honor is in your hands—how loosely you hold it,* she wrote. *The happiness I find in your presence deserts me once I leave you. I have betrayed my marriage vows to come to your bed. This means nothing to you, but everything to me."*

In other letters she writes that she suspects Perkney is seeing another woman. She takes him to task for his faithlessness. I read a passage aloud for Creasy. "If only she knew. He was faithless with a dozen other women."

Creasy cleared his throat. "Perhaps she found out. Poor woman. She must be viewed as having a strong motive to murder the fencing master."

My young minister was having his own problems invading the private thoughts of these women. I heard frequent outbursts of: 'Pernicious rascal' and 'Villainous knave.' He held out one letter to me. "Did you know Perkney signed a pre-contract of marriage with the widow? She believed in his fidelity. She gave herself to him in good faith, and the cur continued to satiate his foul lust with these other women. If she found him out, then she too must be suspect…" In his anger the minister could not go on.

I shook my head. "I think she would sue him for breach of contract. I know Betsy Binning. In the long run such a suit would ruin him, financially and otherwise." Betsy was an intelligent woman. She ran her late husband's tavern with the approval of the selectmen, and managed it well. Of course even the most level headed and capable of women may lose her brains to her loins. I thought of a certain Mohawk in the wilds of the Albany colony. That episode had had near disastrous consequences for me, yet I still longed for his touch...

I opened my third packet of letters, which were tied in white ribbon. These letters were from Caroline Carp, a quiet wren of a woman. I knew her arrogant husband, Major Carp, and could not help but wish her happiness, in even a fleeting moment with the dancing master. I expected timid bleatings of affection. I discovered a Caroline I never knew.

How I long for your touch. My bosoms swell at the thought of your hands encircling them, claiming my soul. I belong to you, O Beloved, you are my conqueror. My body, my heart and my soul are thine. With you inside me I find God. I set down the letter. Creasy should have no look at these words. Even his capacity for forgiveness would be broached. Such blasphemy from the wren... I quite envied her. I glanced over at my companion but he was frowning over a word he mouthed, attempting to decipher its meaning. I snatched up the offending missive and continued reading. Evidently the dancing master had complimented the wren's eyes, for she went on to write: *My eyes are beautiful because they reflect your image, my love, my lover, my true husband.*

Now that would come as a shock to Major Carp, and possibly to Betsy Binning. It struck me that the poor ladies, all of them, must know of the murder by now. How difficult must it be for them, unable as they were to confess their true feelings for the man. Perhaps it would be a kindness for me to visit them and allow them to grieve openly at his loss. I could even recommend Mister Increase Cotton to pray with them and bring them solace. I would assure them that he would keep their secrets, so long as that did not include murder, and it would be to the young minister's honor if he brought even one of them to Redemption. The husbands could not object to a minister's prayers, after all. Perhaps I might myself be the recipient of a murderess' confession. I'm sure it would be all very tearful and touching. And perhaps, if warranted, I could advise them of how best to plead the magistrates. After the course of the Salem witch trails, the Boston magistrates were unwilling to hang women quite so handily.

I picked up yet another letter. This time I was treated to a description of the ways Caroline longed to pleasure her lover with her body. She used her bosoms in an inventive manner, I must say... My own hand strayed to the course fabric of my smock and I caught myself longing for my peach silk robe with its elegant lace sleeves. I felt a spasm of pain. Blue Bear hadn't bedded me since I told him I was with child. Oh, he'd been attentive and concerned, loving and jesting, like an old hen. Just before the birth, Blue Bear and his sister Star Arrow made me swallow gallons of slippery elm bark tea. I drank so much of it, the baby slipped right out with nary a birth pain on my part. I took one look at the slime-covered creature with its shock of black hair and knew I did not want to be a mother. Fortunately my good Dutch friends in Albany were thrilled at the prospect of raising the child. We'd come to an agreement with Blue Bear and his sister, Star—since I was the mother the decision was mine to make, at least in their native way—so the child really had two sets of parents crooning over it. It would speak Dutch and Mohawk before it learned to speak in English. I found I did not worry over its welfare in the least.

Nearby, Creasy was still trying to decipher words and shaking his head. In his own way he'd tried to comfort me for my decision to relinquish the child's care into other hands. He'd pointed out what good parents Anneke and Gerritt would make. "You need not worry about the little mite," he'd said. Since he had kept my secret and stood by me until I'd gone to the Albany colony for the birth, I didn't disillusion him. It wasn't as if I'd rejected the child after all. I'd provided for it in my will. It would be a wealthy little mite.

Reading Caroline Carp's descriptions of her lovemaking made my longing for Blue Bear return threefold. Only Blue Bear was far from Boston. I closed my eyes and leaned back against the velvet hangings of the bed's footboard.

"The brute. The vicious cur." Creasy's cries of outrage startled me. "Do you know how he tortured those poor women?"

My eyes flew open as Creasy strode toward me, shaking a letter in his hand. "It's this English chapel lady...Cecile. Why doesn't she call the magistrates on him? She must have been afraid for her life, and yet she kept on seeing the brute."

"Let me see." I sat up, my interest in the devious fellow rekindling.

Creasy thrust the letter into my face. I took it and read the offending passages. The writing was childlike, slanted and full of loops. Clearly he had misread it. "No. See, she's not writing about physical torture. Some women like to be tied to the bed and, well, teased until she is brought to the full pitch of her lust. Some women like that, Creasy," I said. His face was reddened from his sense of outrage, now it flushed an even deeper crimson.

"It doesn't hurt," I assured him. "He means to delay her gratification until he mounts her and satisfies her desire." The paper dropped from my hands. We both bent to retrieve it and our hands touched. Creasy's eyes were black as coal, his face was on fire. My loins felt his heat in a sudden surge of lust. I threw my arms around his neck and our lips clung together tight as two clamshells. He picked me up and threw back the velvet hangings, falling on top of me on the bed. His hand pulled at the rough smock, raising it over my head while my fingers fumbled to undo his small clothes. I groaned aloud, raising my hips into his.

"Take me now," I commanded. No delayed gratification for me.

"Shall I tie you up?" he asked, a touch of eagerness in his voice.

"No, just take me." It had been so long.

Bam. Bam. Bam. The crashing upon the door startled us so that we nearly fell off the bed. I dived for the curtains at the head of the bed and hid behind them.

Creasy tumbled off the bed and stood there, fumbling with the ties on his small clothes.

"I know you're in there," the voice of Constable Phillymort boomed through the thick wood of the door.

I gave silent thanks to the Lord for the solid strength of that wood.

"Open this door!"

"The letters," I cried. "Don't let him see the letters."

Creasy reached through the curtains and grabbed the packets we'd dropped there. He thrust them at me willy-nilly. I hoped none had fallen to the floor as I stuffed them under the pillows with one hand, while with the other hand I struggled into my smock. Quickly I straightened my petticoats.

Creasy ducked through the curtains. I heard him mumble, "I'm coming, I'm coming." But his steps were quick and going away from the door to the desk. I moved out from the hangings in time to catch more packets he threw at me. These packets were neatly wrapped and tied. I thrust them under the pillows and patted the mass down. Then I sidled over to the foot of the bed where I opened the chest, bent over it and lifted out a number of shirts. "Twelve white shirts," I called out and Creasy bent over the desk to record the number. He straightened and walked with calm steps to the door.

"Six white sheets." I lifted out a bundle as the constable poked his head inside.

"Why did you bar this door?" The constable stalked inside, pounding his staff upon the floor. "'Cleanse thou me from secret faults.' Psalm 14:10."

"As you can see, we are taking inventory here." Creasy spoke in a stiff voice.

I turned to the constable. "Why did you remove the ledger from this chest? You had no right. The entries may tell us who the killer could be." I frowned at the man with my fiercest scowl.

"But we have the villain safe," the constable protested, his voice booming slightly less than usual. He paused.

"I need that ledger," I said. "You are not trained to read it. Bring it to me at once." I stamped my foot.

My attack had its effect. He shifted from foot to foot. "What ledger? I took no ledger. I have seen no ledger. I have not been in this room until this moment, when I heard voices in here." He faltered, leaning over his staff. "My orders were to make the building secure, and that I have done."

"Secure the building, is that what you call it?" I spoke with obvious sarcasm. "When someone has broken in as *we* slept in innocent peace, and stolen the ledger that details the business of the victim? Do you call that securing the building? I'm sure the magistrates will not agree, especially since upon our return Mister Cotton and I had to step over a snoring old watchman." I advanced with what I intended was a threatening step.

"'Man is of trouble as the sparks fly upward.' Job 5:7." The constable shouted these words at me as he beat a hasty retreat.

Creasy barely held in his chuckle until the constable slammed the door behind him.

"The officious old fool," I sputtered.

Creasy held out his hands, fingers upraised. "Don't be angry, Hetty. I was about to do you a wrong. Oh, Blue Bear will kill me if he ever finds out. It's those damned letters, they're dangerous. We have to get rid of them."

I examined the man before me. Whatever was I thinking? All my ardor had vanished with the banging at the door. Perhaps the constable's visit was a Godsend in disguise. I snorted.

"Don't fret over it. Blue Bear won't hatchet you. He's too busy cooing over his son. You'd think it was the first baby ever born." I felt a stab of jealousy in my gut.

Creasy gave me a strange look.

"You're quite right about the letters. I suggest I go about the business of returning them to their rightful owners, providing the owners were not at the murder scene. Do you have any objections to this plan?" I raised my chin, daring him to object.

SIX

I left Creasy to count shirts and walked home to change my clothes. I wouldn't let Mary Ellicott see me dressed as a washerwoman. Besides, visits called for proper attire. In the grim March weather I like to brighten my spirits with a bit of spring color. I chose a robe of cherry-red stripes over a quilted cream petticoat embroidered with green vines. I wore a lace cap beneath a black French hood, hesitating over a cloak of scarlet or a cloak of blue velvet that I'd recently acquired. The ermine-trimmed hood would be the envy of Mistress Ellicott. With reluctance I set aside the blue velvet. Not quite the occasion for ermine.

My first visit must be to Sarah Welsteed, wife of Captain Ezekial Welsteed, a respectable ship's captain who was often away on voyage. Sarah was least on my list of possible murderers. The only worry I found there was the pandemonium of a household of children.

I was shown into a parlor with upended chairs and sheets spread out everywhere. Was it laundry day? Sarah was quick to greet me. I took her outstretched hands.

"Little Thomas has broken his leg jumping from the roof." She squeezed my hands in desperation. "We are building tents to enact the storming of Quebec for him." She gestured to a settee before the hearth where a six-year-old boy lay propped upright by pillows, pelting his five brothers and two sisters with hickory nuts. Children dived for shelter beneath the sheet redoubts.

I paid my respects to the invalid, who looked up at me long

enough to shout, "I am the French defenders," and went on pelting his siblings to cries of pain and hurt. Hickory nuts may be small but their pointed ends are sharp. I wished the attackers better luck than our New England men had under Governor Phips.

"How thoughtful of you to call upon my son," Sarah shouted over the din.

"Sun? No, it's quite overcast this morning, I'm afraid," I yelled back. "I shouldn't be surprised if it snows."

"Oh, we don't know how long it will take for the leg to heal." Sarah shook her head. "The doctor says it may take four weeks."

I gave up conversation and was glad when Sarah beckoned me from the room. I followed her into the kitchen where the smell of nutmeg and cloves filled my nose. Sarah nodded to a stout woman with rosy cheeks. Strands of lank blonde hair hung from a drooping cap.

"She's making a pudding for little Tom's dinner. He has declared he will eat nothing but pudding for his dinner. The doctor says he must keep still, so we give in to him. Sally," she called out to the woman, "will you keep Tom and the children company for a short while? Mrs. Henry has kindly come to call. I'll keep an eye on the pudding for you."

The stout woman waddled out and Sarah dropped onto a bench by the table. She leaned back and closed her eyes. "I'm so tired. Tom broke his leg Monday morning and I sent Sally for the doctor, who was not to be found, so the blacksmith kindly came and set Little Tom's leg until the doctor arrived late in the afternoon. Can you imagine the pain the little boy was in? Yet he bore it quite bravely. The doctor said he could not do any better than the smith in setting the leg, so he gave me a draught for the pain and left us. I don't know what I would have done without Ezekial's sister, for the pain is much worse at night, and that is when she comes to tend him, although Sally couldn't find her, either, on Monday and had to leave a note for her—that is Eliza, you know, Ezekial's sister. Oh dear, I am rambling on, aren't I? And it's so very kind of you to come and ask for his welfare.

The only other person to visit is dear young Mister Mather, who brought the boy a sermon for children and gave Tom a string of rock candy, which all the children enjoyed very much, I assure you, as good Mister Mather taught Tom he must share his good fortune and Tom very naughty-like asked if his brothers and sisters would share in his broken leg..." Sarah shook her head, wiping a loose lock of blond hair in place with the back of a shapely hand.

"Oh dear," I said with real sympathy, "don't you get any sleep?" Sarah had all ready proved she could not have killed the dancing master: Monday was the afternoon of Perkney's death.

"Eliza is upstairs asleep now. In the evening she will get up and watch Tom during the night. If it weren't for her I don't know how I would manage." Sarah straightened her back, looking up at me with a comical twist to her blonde brows. "I'm sorry...can I get you a mug of cider? And please sit down. I've quite forgotten my manners with all the commotion."

I declined the cider but I did take the bench opposite her. "I'll bring you some India tea tomorrow, shall I? Mister Mather says it is very soothing to the spirits. You may wish to share it with the young patient at night. Sarah..." I hesitated, unwilling to add to her troubles, but on the other hand it was my duty to return her property. The packet of letters seemed to burn a hole in my pocket.

"You do know that the fencing master is dead?" I asked.

"Oh, yes. Poor man. Sally says the town talks of nothing else. I was distressed to hear it, and even more distressed to learn that a man of God has been arrested for the crime. Who would think poor Mister Joyliffe capable of such a wicked act?" Sarah raised bewildered blue eyes to me. "To think my dear boy was laying here in pain and Mister Joyliffe was out murdering a good man. Mister Joyliffe should have been here, comforting my Thomas. I was quite upset about it, I can tell you."

"Was he a good man, this Mister Perkney?" I asked, watching her face. "You took dancing lessons from him, I believe."

"Oh, yes. I did. I thought him a kind and courteous gentleman. Poor man." Her eyelids flickered and dropped.

I pulled the packet of letters from my petticoat pocket and pushed them across the table. "I would advise you to burn these," I said.

She turned the packet around and around in her hands. "Oh dear." She spoke with a reflective air. "I have been so occupied with Thomas I've had no chance to mourn the poor man as I should."

"Rest assured that no one has seen these letters but me, and I will tell no one. You may count upon my discretion. Mister Increase Cotton and I have been asked to look into the murder of the gentleman."

"Oh. Yes, of course. With a minister involved, I should have known." Sarah's voice faltered.

The lady did not seem to hold such strong feelings for the late fencing master that she would break down in tears at my questioning, so I went on. "What was he like?"

"What was he like?" Sarah repeated the question. She pondered for a moment before answering. Her pretty mouth titled in a slight curve. "Francis was charming and attentive. He had a strong arm and a good leg, although I thought his face plain. That is, until he smiled. What wouldn't a woman do to see that smile. It lit up his face like the sun. Hetty, I don't know if you can understand…"

I nodded. Perhaps it was a good thing the woman didn't know me that well.

"At first it was his strong arm around me in the dance, and oh…he kissed my hand that very first lesson and every lesson after. There was something about the way he did it—I can't explain. Then it was a whisper in my ear, his lips making me shiver, and then his hand grazed my bosom, and before I knew it I was in his bed. And in the daylight, too. I think I liked that the best of all." Sarah's face glowed as she spoke.

I felt a pang of envy. Why hadn't I taken up dancing lessons?

"Oh, the sheer bliss of falling asleep in his arms in the afternoon, and when I woke, he was there telling me how beautiful I looked. A woman does like to hear such words, Hetty. In the afternoon...to have the leisure to fall asleep in the afternoon." She sighed and I sighed with her.

I left Sarah Welsteed seated at the kitchen table, lost in a reverie of quiet and peace. I hoped the pudding would not burn. My second visit must be to the home of Caroline Carp, another lady who surprised me when I heard her name upon blind Henry's lips. Had it been the name of her husband, I could not have been more amazed.

Major Caleb Carp, so far as I knew, had never raised his saber in battle, but he had donated the funds to equip a company of militia. Major Carp's company was known for its precision marching across the green on Training Day. It had won medals, with the men carrying their half-pikes like a row of fence posts. The major kept a fine house on Cotton Hill, with a fine orchard in the back. Trees of apple, cherry and peach stood at stiff attention in neat rows. Even the untidy pumpkin curbed its urge to sprawl, growing fat and plump in the major's garden on a short vine. The major's pumpkins were the largest in Boston.

Caroline Carp was the major's third wife and a congregant of Cousin Cotton Mather's church. Cousin Cotton frequently praised her for her good works, holding her out as an example to his wife, my cousin Abigail. As if Abigail didn't have enough to do raising his children, keeping a welcoming home for a man prominent in religious, political and community affairs, and in meeting her husband's every whim as if at the command of Moses.

It was Creasy's praise of Caroline Carp that earned my respect. She provided work for many of the poor women of his church. She set the wives and widows to spinning, knitting, washing, and sewing for her. These tasks gave them needed pennies for the family. Caroline also bought their baskets of freshly picked wild berries and cranberries. Their buckets of oysters and clams fed the Carp table. Their knitted mittens graced the hands of the well-off members of the Mather church. She also solicited garments for the cold winter months from Second Church to clothe and warm Creasy's Summer Street church members.

Could such a little paragon of charity turn in cold fury and murder a man—especially a lover? Caroline Carp, who reminded me of nothing so much as a little wren, timid and unassuming, going about her business while birds of greater beauty drew the attention? I found it difficult to imagine a blood-dripping sword in those tiny hands. I shook my head at the thought. Nonetheless, I must make this painful visit.

SEVEN

I was surprised when the major answered the door himself, his lank frame and hound-like face blocking the sparse March sunlight from profaning his home. This was not good, I thought to myself. I needed to speak to Caroline alone. However, civility must be maintained, so I extended my hand. "Major, how nice to see you here. I have come to speak to Caroline. Is she within?"

The major bowed, giving my fingers a peck. As he straightened a lock of stringy brown hair escaped from the black ribbon that held it back. The lock fell across his sunken cheek, where it stuck. Now here was a gentleman who should wear a periwig, thought I, having observed a pink bald spot on the top of his head.

"My wife is ill. She is not receiving visitors today."

He stood like a stone monolith, with no intention of allowing me inside, not even into the hall. Now I could picture this man killing the dancing master, but it wouldn't be in passion. It would be with cold deliberation. And he knew how to use a sword. I hesitated a moment, gathering my courage.

"Oh…then I am glad I have come. Perhaps I may be of service? Have you sent the maid for a doctor? Shall I sit with her until he comes? I'm sure a busy man like you has other occupations besides answering the door," I said, attempting to be genuine in my desire to help. If he was trying to stop me from speaking to his wife I felt equal to the challenge.

The major scowled down at me. "I answer the door because the girl has run away. Pernicious jade. She's run off with one of my wife's handkerchiefs."

"Oh, poor man. Servants. So unreliable nowadays. And you are left all by yourself to tend to a sick wife. Poor man," I repeated, the germ of an idea in my mind. Most men are afraid of catching an illness. They'd rather be shot by a musket bullet. "Has she the rheum? I hear it is sweeping the town—very infectious, it is. Is she pale? Does she have a fever? Does her head hurt? For these are the symptoms, I assure you. A nasty rheum, and she will need all the handkerchiefs she possesses with it. Very infectious. It's very bad of the servant to run off." I babbled on, telling symptoms of the disease. "Does she refuse food? Or drink?"

Major Carp stepped back, his brows raised in concern. "Why yes, those are indeed the symptoms she displays."

I clicked my tongue in sympathy. "Are you not expected to train your company, poor man?" I asked. The major's company of militia seemed to be his reason for being.

The gentleman jerked his head in a nod, his lower lip drooping. "She will not have a doctor. There is no help for it, I must stay with her."

"Ah but there is a duty you owe to your men. I hear that Harry Kegleigh's company prepares in extra time for next Training Day, hoping to best you." At the gentleman's snort of contempt for his rival, I laid my hand lightly upon his sleeve. "Oh, he shan't beat you for the medal, I am sure of it. But we must take no chances, mustn't we? I know my own duty, and I must certainly keep your wife company while you attend to the Town's affairs. Perhaps I can make her a draught—an herbal infusion to lessen the fever. Hyperion tea. That would be just the thing. Will you allow me to attend to her?" I placed my gloved hands together and looked beseechingly into his face. I thought I truly knew what ailed the lady, and I could bring her some comfort, if only by allowing her to speak of the late dancing master.

"Well…" The major craned his neck, his eyes scanning the road as if he expected his militiamen to march down it. "I do have commitments."

"Ah, that's settled then," I smiled at the man and pushed past him into the hallway. "Don't you worry, Sir. I shall stay with her until she is settled for the evening."

"She's in the parlor." He directed me with the toss of a long arm. Before I could answer, the door slammed and I was left alone in the hallway. That was easily done.

Caroline Carp sat huddled by the hearth, a silk shawl wrapped around her head and shoulders. She did not look up when I entered the room. Her gaze was fixed upon the flames of the hearth fire. I cleared my throat. She did not turn.

"Caroline!" My call drew her attention. The face that turned to me was ghostly pale, with the eyes of a startled doe. "Merciful Lord, you are ill." And I'd thought her husband told me a story to keep me from seeing her. I rushed to her, my hand held out to prevent her from rising. "Your husband saw me in. He said you were ill. I offered to keep you company. I'm afraid I encouraged him to go out for a bit," I knew I was speaking too fast but I could not help myself.

"Have you sent for a doctor? I know an excellent young man. I'll get him for you," I offered. At this point she had half-risen from her bench by the fire. I laid my hand upon her shoulder and that slight pressure was enough to force her back onto the bench.

"Hetty. I knew you must come."

Her voice was calm but it rose from a disembodied spirit. The hair on the back of my neck prickled. She was but a little woman to begin with. The shawl enshrouded her and an emaciated face looked up at me.

"No doctor. The major worries too much. Come and sit next to me." She patted the hard wooden settle beside her and handed me a crewelwork pillow. Her fingers were thin and delicate. "I'm sorry, I'm forgetting my manners. May I get you a mug of cider?" She lifted her hand and the fingers shook like the wings of a captured bird. "We have no serving girl to wait upon us. Major Carp frightened her away. He frightens them all away."

I could not help an exclamation and she looked at me in surprise. "He doesn't mean to, it's his voice. He speaks in a loud voice. It's natural with him. It will only take a moment. I'll get you that cider." She began to rise, the shawl slipping from her head and slithering down her shoulders. Caroline did not notice.

I grabbed her sleeve and pulled her back. "No cider, thank you, my dear, but I will take a cherry brandy, and so will you. I'll get it. I know where it is." I handed her my cushion and she held it in her lap, turning it round and round.

At the sideboard I poured out two tumblers of red-amber liquid and carried them to the settle. One I handed to her and stood over her until she took a good sip. I seated myself beside her and drank from my own tumbler. The liquid felt sweet and thick on my throat, warmth coursed through my veins. I hoped it would bring a bit of color back into the woman's cheeks. I know it certainly helped me. How could I question a sick woman about a murder? Perhaps if she would agree to see a doctor, I could try after she'd been treated. I decided to hint at the possibility.

"I just came from the home of Sarah Welsteed. Her young son has broken his leg. What utter chaos. The other children are running around like mad dogs and the little boy lies on a couch ordering everyone about." I shook my head at the folly of bearing children.

"The six-year-old? That would be Thomas." Caroline's dark eyes grew moist. "What pain the poor lad must feel." Her thin lips quivered.

The woman looked as if she were in deep pain herself.

"Are you sure you won't see a doctor?" I asked. "I've found Geoffrey Malbone to be of surpassing competence and complete discretion. A woman needs a physician she can trust, don't you agree?" I placed my hand over her thin, cold fingers. "I've found I could trust Doctor Malbone completely." Although I'd once suspected him of murder, but I did not tell her that.

"No, thank you, Hetty." She sighed. "I'm just tired…so very tired." Her shoulders slumped.

I picked up the shawl and tied its ends around her shoulders. "There. You must not stand upon ceremony with me, my dear. May I help you to your bed? I'll see you settled and take my leave." I would return when the woman felt in better health. Caroline Carp in this condition was incapable of harming a fly.

The woman shook her head. "If I go to bed now, I shan't be able to sleep tonight." She lifted the thick glass of brandy to her lips. "I must sleep tonight."

"Caroline." I hesitated. There was another form of medicine that often affected a cure. "Would you like to speak to Mister Mather? Cousin Cotton is quite knowledgeable about herbal infusions. He may be able to prescribe a strengthening tonic for you." Most ministers knew how to cure the body as well as the soul, and perhaps praying with the minister of her church would be of more help than anything else. Whatever her relationship with the dancing master, confessing her sin would relieve her of her guilt, and one thing about Cousin Cotton—such confessions were kept in the strictest of confidence. He could be discreet when necessary.

Caroline's slight frame shook like an aspen in a breeze. "No. No. Not Mister Mather. Please." She turned a strained face to me.

I could not blame her. For many people it was not easy to speak to Cousin Cotton. Some were in awe of him; others were tongue-tied around him. One did not care to disappoint such a saintly man with one's sin-prone human nature. To his due, Cousin Cotton is most sincere in tending to his flock like a good shepherd. But would I confess my sins to him? Well, I might, but only to shock him. It is wrong of me, I know, but I do delight in shocking Cotton Mather. To see the wrinkles in the high brow, the puckering of the long mouth, the moisture gather in the sanctimonious eyelids, the sight brings wicked pleasure into my heart. This would not do for the lady before me. I suggested another, more palatable alternative.

"You know Mister Increase Cotton," I said. "He is a good man. Should you like to speak to him?"

"I thought he would be here, with you." Her eyes were black and moist.

I was taken by surprise. "Why did you think that?" I was curious. Creasy and I were not joined at the hip, by any means. I had my mercantile interests and my farm in Rumney Marsh to keep me occupied. He had his flock at Summer Street Church. We were both cousins of Cotton Mather—I by Mather's marriage to my cousin Abigail, and Creasy by birth, and upon occasion we met there, but most often we came together when a crises threatened Cousin Cotton Mather's peace of mind. Then he would send for Creasy, and his wife Abigail would send for me.

Caroline gave me a strange look. The cordial must have given her some confidence. "Everyone knows you two are looking into the murder, that the ministers of Boston have asked you to do so."

I cursed under my breath. We had just begun to question people, and yet the word was out. Men and women alike are less likely to speak freely if they realize they are suspects in a murder. Besides which, it is difficult enough to question your friends. They resent you for thinking them capable of such a great evil, especially if they are guilty.

"Isn't that why you are here?" Caroline looked at me with those enormous dark eyes.

I sputtered, at a loss for words. Of course I had come to speak to her about the letters, which even now seemed to burn like fire in my pocket. I had not come to badger a sick woman about her relationship with the dancing master. I did not come to judge her. Who was I to judge any woman in her position? I did wish to clear her, however, and to return her letters so she could destroy them…or savor them, as she wished.

Caroline leaned back against the wooden settle. She clutched her hands in her lap, her dark eyes haunted. "Well, you need look no further for your murderer. I killed him."

"You killed him?" I repeated the words, but I did not believe them. "How did you do it?"

She turned her head away. "I don't want to talk about it. You may call the constable now." She waved a shaking hand. "I should prefer to be arrested while my husband is absent, please."

EIGHT

Mister Increase Cotton, minister to the poor congregation of widows, sailors, laborers and orphans of the Summer Street Church, quaffed a deep dip from the rum punch bowl, the brew courtesy of his friend, M'sieur Germaine, the Huguenot merchant. They sat in the conviviality of the Dog and Pot in the company of one Joshua Stebbins, a merchant whose spices and shrub were no doubt gracing the very punch they drank. The Dog and Pot was a meeting place to check up on the shipping lists, to listen to political gossip or to enjoy the eel pie and the special brews mine host concocted. It was also the place to collect tidbits of information concerning the late dancing master, Francis Perkney. Creasy hardly had to ask. Men came straight to him eager to share their recollections, no doubt hoping to learn a new detail about the bloody deed to carry to the next tavern.

"Say, did ye find out why the young minister ran the rascal through?" asked one. "Defending himself, most like. That Perkney's been in trouble with the justices since he come here, I tell ye. Fined him twice, they did." The man gave a self-satisfied nod.

Creasy pursed his lips. The man only thought what others thought. He made a careful answer. "We should not be too hasty to judge." He spoke in his best ministerial tone. "As you say, the dancing master was troublesome. Surely there were others with reason to harm him."

"Oh yes." The man grinned. "Half the husbands in town, I hear. There's old Biggins, sent his clerk to spy on that young wife of his. Made him walk her to dancing lessons twice a week, he did, and walk her home again. The wife run off with the clerk, she did."

The spice merchant chuckled aloud while M'sieur snorted behind his hand. Creasy sighed at the vanity of old age.

"Old Biggins is more concerned for the loss of his clerk," the man added. He mimicked the old man in a quavering voice. "I shan't give him a reference, I shan't."

Even Creasy had to smile at this. Perhaps old Biggins might blame the dancing master for the loss of his young wife, but since Biggins was a frail eighty-three years of age, he could not be the killer. With a wave of his hand the man walked away to another table.

Creasy felt stymied by all the talk he'd heard about jealous husbands. This meant that anyone he questioned about the actions of either John Ellicot or Major Caleb Carp would immediately connect the men as suspects in the murder. Creasy did not wish to brand any man at this point, nor to cause any more speculation from the public. Nor did he wish to bring the names of the wives into it. Perhaps the women had sinned, but they must be given the chance to achieve redemption for their sins. The days of wearing a large A upon their clothing to denote adultery were long gone, and the Bay Colony the better for it. Repentance must be sincere, not forced upon one through a public shaming, at least that's what he ministered. Creasy understood that the primitive conditions faced by his grandfathers in settling this wilderness colony called for strict discipline. With a sense of pride he thought of the prosperity and growth Massachusetts Bay had achieved in this year of 1694, a blessing from the Lord and the hard work of his neighbors. Men like M'sieur, who had to flee his country with only the clothes upon his back, and of Mister Stebbins, the spice merchant, sitting beside him.

Stebbin spoke up, his tone implying a question. "The sailors say that warehouse is haunted. When they row out to the ships early of a morn they say they've seen shapes on the wharf that are there one moment and disappear the next."

M'sieur nodded. "I've heard that, too. My foreman was a sailor and he sneaks off to the wharf every chance he gets. He told me they think the evil spirits killed the dancing master and placed the sword in the minister's hand so he would be blamed for it. The devils don't like our Reformed faith because it is so strong."

"Yes, and strange lights have been seen—like will-o-wisps—but in late fall and early spring when such things do not occur." Stebbins leaned over the table, towards Creasy. He spoke in a low tone. "In the old days they hung pirates off that spit of land."

"I've heard it's the souls of those who drowned in a shipwreck outside the harbor." M'sieur also lowered his voice.

"Gentlemen, these are tales of ignorant, superstitious sailors. Think of the harm such tales cause. Remember Salem town. We'll have no such superstitious gossip in Boston. Are we not men of science and learning?"

"Well, of course I don't believe what a few old sailors say after a night of ale and rum." Stebbins leant back in his chair, tapping one finger upon the table.

"Forgive me, but I have seen the spirit of a woman after her foul murder. Oh, my good and just Lord, spare me from such a sight again." The Huguenot merchant removed a square of linen from his coat pocket and rubbed it across his sweating forehead.

Creasy leaned over, patting the merchant's sleeve. What the Frenchman had seen was a scandalous prank played by Hetty Henry, but Creasy could not tell M'sieur this. And Hetty had paid for her foolish prank; she'd nearly lost her life. He soothed the merchant. "Now M'sieur, you know we caught the lady's murderer. You will not see her spirit again. I have prayed upon it, and I'm certain the lady's soul is at rest." Creasy's hand remained upon the merchant's sleeve in a gesture of comfort. He enjoyed the company of the Huguenot merchant and looked forward to dinner the following night, as offered by the obliging gentleman. M'sieur had agreed to invite the two Englishwomen who were among Perkney's conquests to attend, so that Creasy and Hetty could meet them. Creasy quite looked forward to making the acquaintance of those ladies who wrote such salacious letters.

"It's not women's spirits the sailors saw, anyhow," Stebbins said, injecting his knowledge. "It's clear they are male spirits, and they carry heavy things like pirates' chests and such. That's why the sailors think it's the souls of those pirates who were gibbeted on the spit. I'm only repeating what they say," he added, his tone defensive. "Too much rum and ale, no doubt, but that's what they say."

"Oh, frightful. I do not like this." M'sieur held the square of linen to his forehead.

"Now M'sieur, don't pay any attention to these tales. The man had a troublesome reputation." Creasy scowled a warning at Stebbins. "No doubt the dancing master was up to some mischief late at night, when all good men of Boston were asleep in their beds." As he spoke he recalled Henry's belief that men frequented Perkney's rooms during the night. He'd have to look into it. Perhaps Hetty could use her sources with the waterfront rats she knew only too well. If there were any shady goings-on, she'd find out. His thoughts were interrupted from a voice that spoke from behind his chair.

"We all know who killed Perkney. The ministers hated him—you preached against him, you hounded him and plotted to drive him out of town. When that didn't rid you of the man, yon Joyliffe snuck in like a thief and murdered the poor man."

Creasy swiveled in his chair. Rufus Catesby was a wiry, fox-haired man, a joyner noted for his fox-like business sense. Catesby had been a follower of the former Royal Governor, Edmund Andros, therefore he was no friend to the Mathers, who were instrumental in sending that corrupt official in chains to London. Catesby stood there, hands upon his thin hips, while a burly gaptoothed companion grinned beside him.

Creasy decided to ignore both men. He turned back to M'sieur, whose thick brows were raised in astonishment at the audacity of the laborer.

"Surely you don't accuse my friend Mister Cotton, here, of

being involved in such a preposterous plot?" M'sieur Germaine addressed the newcomer.

"It is a preposterous idea. Don't pay any attention to him, Sir." That was Creasy's advice, which he fully intended to follow himself.

"And wasn't it a Mather sermon found beside the dead body?" Catesby refused to be ignored, raising his voice so that all heads turned in their direction.

Creasy's fist curled into a ball at the sneering tone. His thin black brows gathered into a frown. The man could attack him all he liked, but accuse his uncle, Increase Mather? That would not do, not at all. Increase Mather was not responsible if a frightened colleague dropped a printing of one of his sermons. Many people carried copies of Uncle Increase's sermons. Yet this man Catesby would reframe an accident as a murderous plot. Such a slur upon the good name of Mather could not go unchallenged.

M'sieur intervened. "I beg you to consider my friend's feelings, Sir," he said.

"I don't want no trouble with the Mather cub." Catesby flung freckled hands into the air. He shrugged narrow shoulders.

"My name is Mister Cotton to you, Sir." Creasy spoke through tight lips.

"Cotton. Mather. What difference? The father, the son, and the unholy trinity, I say." The fox-green eyes sparkled, the narrow chin jutted out in challenge.

Creasy rose from his chair. "I am a minister of the Lord and will be respected as such." He spoke in a cool voice. To those who knew him, that calm was far more dangerous than fiery words. The tone meant that he held his anger well in hand but was ready to act.

"As a minister or as a murderer?" Catesby drawled the words, leaning forward upon his the tips of his boots. "Or as a coward who will stab a man in the back?"

With his reddish hair flying about, the man looked like a crowing rooster. Creasy had a mind for a chicken dinner. With a sudden movement, shrugging himself out of his coat and his biscuit-colored waistcoat, he began to roll up his sleeves.

"Come, come, gentlemen," M'sieur spoke in some alarm. He thrust his sword in its golden-scrolled scabbard between the two men.

"Oh, yon minister is brave when there's a crowd of people to protect him." Catesby thin lips curled into sneer. "Come out in the alley and see what he's made of."

"You think I won't? Here." Creasy turned, handing his coat to the Huguenot gentleman. "Hold this for me, if you will, Sir. It's too good to sully on the likes of him." He nodded to Catesby.

"But…but, Mister Cotton, Sir, you will not brawl in the streets with this ruffian?" M'sieur sputtered out the words, his round face flushed with worry.

Creasy moved towards the door. "No, I'll brawl in the alley. The man must be taught a lesson."

A crowd piled out of the front door and scurried around the building, following Creasy and his challenger. A layer of clamshells paved the alley next to the tavern. Catesby's followers filed to the back, leaving a space in the middle, while other men blocked the alleyway from public view of the street.

The two men circled each other, boots crunching upon the shells. Creasy landed the first punch, a quick jab at Catesby's nose, followed by a left hook to the jaw that sent the slight man into the arms of his companion with the gap tooth. Gap-tooth shoved his burden back at Creasy. Catesby threw his arms around Creasy's waist and butted him in the mid-section. Creasy swept his boot around Catesby's leg and the fox-faced man fell to the ground, dragging Creasy with him. The crowd buzzed like a hive of angry bees.

Both men puffed from the impact with the ground and with each other's fists. They rolled around on the sharp clamshells, the edges nicking flesh with more success than the blows each tried to land. The young minister tried to pin his opponent facedown but Catesby was slippery as an eel. He rolled from Creasy's grasp with a knee in the groin in passing. Catesby attempted to rise to one knee. Creasy grabbed his shirt and pulled him back down. Catesby's head made a loud smacking sound as it crunched into the shell-covered ground.

Shrill whistles from the alley corner alerted the mob to the coming of the watch. Creasy felt hands drag him from his prey, lift him to his feet and carry him away from Catesby. He struggled to get back at his opponent but suddenly realized Catesby was being dragged down the alley away from him. Rough hands escorted him back into the tavern, forcing him into a chair. His coat was thrust at him with a shrill whisper: "Put this on. Put this on."

M'sieur plunked his stout body in the next chair, making frantic gestures at him while other hands brushed bits of clam shell from his shirt. M'sieur fluttered a handkerchief in Creasy's face, mimicking the act of wiping. Creasy took it and wiped off droplets of blood, leaving dots of red on the white linen. He stared at the dots, noting with pride that he'd lost so little blood in the fray. M'sieur was whispering something to him about the watch and someone handed him a glass of amber liquid. He took a good slug, gasping as the fire burned its way down his throat. It felt good. He set down the glass and swept back a clump of loose black hair from his cheek. A black ribbon dangled down his neck. He grabbed it and fastened his hair in place with a bow. Creasy wore his hair in a natural manner. Not for him the fashionable great periwig of Cousin Cotton Mather. M'sieur nodded in approval.

By the time the gold-knobbed staff of the constable pounded upon the tavern door, a crowd of men sat in serene comfort around their respective tables, glass or mug in hand. The innkeeper escorted the dour-faced constable into the premises.

"Disturbance?" The innkeeper's voice rose in wonder. "What disturbance? As you can see for yourself, Sir, there has been no disturbance on these premises. I keep an orderly house, Sir. No gaming, no cards, no disturbances. Won't tolerate it."

Ten minutes after the constable left the Dog and Pot—with the admonition: 'How long wilt thou be drunken? Put away thy wine from thee.' Samuels 1:14—Creasy rose from his seat and sauntered out the door. His previous good mood dissipated by the constable's visit, he berated himself for his pugnacious behavior. The appropriate reaction, he reasoned, would have been to pity Catesby for his unhappy nature, to keep his own temper in check, and to walk away from provocation…after offering to pray with the man. What an example to set for his congregation. Instead of prayers and guidance, he offered blows. Creasy vowed to reflect upon soft answers and to preach about turning cheeks at the Sunday service. He would confess his unruly temper to his congregation of rough sailors, worn laborers and penniless widows. With their loyal natures, he was certain they would forgive him. But could he forgive himself?

Unconscious of the long strides he took, Creasy covered three long blocks before he was aware of the patter of little feet behind him. In actual fact, it was the tug upon his coattails that alerted him to the presence of the ragged fellow in the tattered cloak behind him.

Creasy's abrupt stop very nearly caused a collision. The man pulled up, teetering upon wobbly legs. "Mister Cotton…" The man panted for a few seconds, his breath coming out in clouds of frosty air. "Mister Cotton," he repeated.

The little man's nose was bright with cold or rum, Creasy wasn't sure which. He noted the fellow's thin, waxy lips, the moth-eaten wool cap upon greasy hair of an indeterminate color, the pale blue eyes rimmed with red. Gnarled fingers peeping from half-mittens were blue-white from cold.

Creasy made a quick assessment, speaking in a curt tone, "If you come with me to the church, I can trade you a good warm cloak and a new pair of mittens for your own garments." His ladies would wash and fashion the old scraps into something useful, he knew, and Cousin Cotton's church were really quite generous in sharing their cast-offs with the Summer Street church of needier Christians. Several years ago he'd received a sizable sum of money that must have come from a benefactor of the Mather's church, one who insisted upon anonymity. Cousin Cotton claimed he did not know who it was. The donation kept his people warm and fed for two winters now. The little man before him wasn't a member of his church, but he was in need.

Creasy resumed his stride, assuming the fellow would follow. The fellow did, and once more he felt a tug upon his coattails.

"Mister Cotton. Mister Cotton, Sir. Stay a bit, will ye?" The man puffed out the request.

The fellow held on to the coattail so that once more Creasy was obliged to stop. He felt some annoyance—why didn't the odd creature just come along and collect his offerings? It wasn't as if Creasy had the reputation for making a man beg for a helping hand, nor would he force the fellow to kneel in long prayer or make him labor for the goods. Creasy frowned.

"Come along, Fellow. The clothes are yours for the taking."

"But Mister Cotton, Sir… It's about Rufus Catesby." The little man took a deep breath. "Not but what I'd welcome a warm cloak, Sir, and the mittens…"

Creasy nodded. "They are yours, good sir. Now, what about Catesby?"

"Ye bested him in the fight, ye know it. Well, the constable says as we are to tell if we know anything at all about the murder of the dancing master." The little man paused to puff out clouds of frozen air.

Creasy's shoulders straightened in sudden interest. He made himself curb his impatience until the fellow caught his breath. The cold didn't bother him; March meant the coming of spring. Once the temperature rose above freezing Creasy felt himself coming alive again, buoyant with the hint of warmth in the air.

"Not that I know about the murder. I ain't saying I do, Mister. Don't think it, I beg ye."

Creasy heard the wheeze in the man's throat and felt concern. He held up one hand to prevent the man from speaking. "I have an infusion of horehound and hyssop that will help you with that throat of yours. I'll give you a bottle." Ministers were often called upon to cure the body as well as the soul. Most of his colleagues were skillful in their uses of herbal medicines.

The little man's head bobbed in enthusiastic agreement. "I just do my duty, Mister Cotton, Sir," he said, resuming his narrative. "After I seen ye pin that man, that Catesby—and ye done it fair and square, I say—it reminded me of what I seen."

Creasy waited while the man coughed. Spittle ran down the weathered lips.

"I seen Rufus Catesby having words with that fancy dancin' master just last week, I did. I was comin' around the corner of Fish Street when I heard some awful cuss words and there's Catesby, shakin' his fist at the dancin' man. I couldn't help hearin' the words, Sir, they was shouted out so loud." The little man's shoulders shook from a sudden bout of coughing. He put a dirty hand up to a scraggly throat that appeared shaven in patches.

"Come to the church and take that infusion before you try to speak, Sir," Creasy said, thinking that he must curb his impatience a little longer. What were those words Catesby said to the late dancing master? Had they led to Perkney's death? Creasy's heartbeat quickened at the thought that Rufus Catesby might have killed Perkney. What a burden that must lift from poor Jacob Joyliffe. Yet he'd wait to hear the words that might convict another man, the poor old fellow before him needed medical attention as well as warm clothing.

The man took deep breaths; he stopped coughing. "Thank ye, kindly, Mister Cotton. I'll come along with ye, and that gladly. Let me just tell ye this. Catesby said as he would pay an extra two pounds if the dancin' man would give him another two weeks on his debt. That's what he said, Sir, and whatever the fancy man said to him, he weren't happy. He shouted and cursed some more so that I turned 'round and went back the way I come. I didn't want no trouble."

The little man began to cough again. Creasy patted him upon his back. "Did you hear what the dancing master said to Catesby?" He could not help asking the question, even though he wished the fellow would just follow him to the church.

"Couldn't hear, Sir. Spoke too low, cool as can be, he was. Catesby was yellin' and waving his fists around. Dancin' man just stood there." The fellow hugged himself, shivering beneath the tattered cloak.

"Come on, then." Creasy gestured and the poor man fell into step. Creasy reminded himself to shorten his stride. He felt so elated at the information, he felt like running the rest of the way home. So, Catesby owed the dancing master a sum sufficient to add two pounds to it for an extension of the loan. Would Catesby murder to free himself from that debt? Perhaps in anger he might. Surely the wound that killed the dancing master had been struck in anger. Wait until Hetty heard about this new information. They'd meet to exchange thoughts this evening at supper. Up to this moment he'd nothing new to tell her, now he might be able to present her with the murderer.

NINE

Creasy gave me a critical look as I slouched into Milk's Tavern and dropped into the chair opposite. "What?" I asked with irritation I could not conceal. I was aware of my red face, the strands of hair escaped from my hood and that I gritted my teeth. Creasy was half-bent over the table, as he'd started to rise at my approach. Now he straightened.

"I've never seen you looking frazzled before. Frustrated, flummoxed and even forlorn, but never frazzled. You are usually a vision of spring." He made a gentlemanly bow.

It's a good thing he added the compliment. Even so, I'm afraid I was a bit waspish. "Well you don't look so good yourself. You've got a large bruise on your cheek and you've torn your cuff. The lace is dirty. What have you been up to?"

"Upholding the honor of the Cottons and the Mathers." He grinned at me. "I didn't have time to change. Sorry," he added, looking down and fingering a piece of torn lace.

"Let's eat." I motioned to the landlord for service. I would feel better with some nourishment, then I could contend with his nonsense. Upholding the honor of the Cottons and the Mathers indeed. Why who would even question such a thing?

Creasy plunked himself down in his chair. He leaned forward to address me. "I must tell you my news." He paused for a second, eyeing me like a small boy who'd caught a frog. "I may have found the killer of Francis Perkney."

"Oh, is that all?" I yawned, covering my mouth with a belated hand. "I've found two of them."

Ignoring the gentleman's open mouth, I opened mine for a bowl of thick and creamy fish chowder. Thick slices of rye and cornmeal bread with fresh butter, and a tankard of cider helped to soothe the turmoil in my guts. The wrenching emotions I'd witnessed today had left me…well, frazzled. How could these women become so entangled with a man not their husbands that they would grieve themselves into their graves? It was a great puzzle to me. Further, they would lie about their role in his death. As if their very love for him was so potent it could kill. I'd lost two husbands, myself, but I never thought my love had killed either of them. My brave young Jack died in a battle at sea. My second husband, my Mister Henry, died from a heart complication, not so unusual for a man in his sixty-fifth year. Such is God's will and one must accept it.

I washed down the last bite of bread with the last swallow of cider. With the clunk of the empty tankard upon the table, I dropped my spoon and concentrated upon the events of the day.

I began with Sarah Welsteed's son and the fact she hadn't left his side on the day of the dancing master's death. There were witnesses, including the doctor and the sister-in-law. Then I told Creasy of Carolyn Carp's confession.

"She didn't kill Master Perkney, the silly goose. She didn't even know how he died. She said she stabbed him through the heart with a knife because they'd quarreled. I think she is protecting her husband. Perhaps she thinks he killed Perkney. Have you found out where the major was that afternoon?"

At Creasy's negative nod I went on, ignoring his stutter. Whatever he was going to say fell upon deaf ears and a mouth that was determined to narrate my day. I couldn't help myself. My tongue insisted upon relieving itself of the frustration I'd felt and been unable to express until now.

"At least Carolyn had a measure of control over her behavior." I frowned at the memory of my next visit. "Mary Ellicot was in great distress." I continued my tale. "I no sooner walked into the room when the lady screamed out that I was come to arrest her. Now you know we have no authority to arrest anybody, Creasy. Could I explain that to her? No. She would not listen to reason. She fell over onto her couch as if in a swoon and began to babble about how it was all her fault, that she'd killed him and was doomed to burn in the fires of Hell for all Eternity..." I shook my head. "And she looked like a creature from Hell, Creasy, if you'll forgive me for speaking so. You know how Mary Ellicot flaunts her wealth with her lace-trimmed gowns and gold-trimmed petticoats—well, I could afford those trimmings, too, but I don't go down to the wharves in them or parade about the streets in all my finery the way she does. Sheer vanity, and not even becoming to her as tall and gawky as she is..."

At Creasy's look of disapproval I held up my hand to signify my repentance. "I know. It's not charitable of me to speak of her so. I'm sorry. The poor woman was really in a state and I should not mock her. Her gown was soiled and wrinkled, as if she'd slept in her clothes for days, and her face was ghostly white." I paused, biting my tongue. On a recent occasion I'd dressed up like a ghost and it almost ended in disaster. But the lady did remind me of my own ghost-painted face, only her face wasn't painted. "Her eyes were red-rimmed from weeping and her hair hung uncombed... Ugh." I closed my eyes, shivering at the recollection. "I did feel sorry for her, but you couldn't talk to the woman. She was beyond reason. Eliza Welsteed was there, you know, Captain Welsteed's sister. Mistress Welsteed was most concerned about Mrs. Ellicott and did not care to leave her alone, so I said I would stay with her while Mistress Welsteed went to find a neighbor lady. I must endure two hours of whining and moaning before she returned." I threw up my hands. "I was never..."

"The poor woman," Creasy said, his black brows furrowed in sympathy. "Did she confess to the murder of the dancing master?"

"Well, in a manner of speaking she did, but one couldn't make sense of the woman. I didn't believe her for a minute when she raved that it was her fault. No, I think it is unhinging her mind that her husband may have taken his revenge upon the dancing master. The guilt she feels is depriving her of reason." In my gut I felt that Mary Ellicott was not the murderer.

"Shall I go pray with the woman? Perhaps it would comfort her—at least I can try."

Creasy had a way with wayward females, that I knew. However, the lady's own minister was Cousin Cotton—Cotton Mather of Second Church—and Cousin Cotton had an absolute gift for consoling desolate women. I tried to explain this to my companion without hurting his feelings. "It's known all over town that you and I are looking into this murder. If the woman thought I was come to arrest her, she'll think the same of you. It will upset her even more. Perhaps you could put a word in Cousin Cotton's ear that one of his parishioners needs his aid." I left it at that.

Creasy nodded. "Yes, I will do just that. Cousin Cotton has a special gift for soothing sensitive females, I must admit. I shall go direct to him. Now, before I leave, let me tell you—"

I held up my hand to stop him, wanting to complete my own tale. "By the time Mistress Welsteed returned I was ready to pull out my hair. I'd taken the opportunity to hand her letters over to the woman. Mary Ellicott hugged the letters to her breast and moaned and cried and kissed my hands for being so good." I stopped my narrative again, shuddering at the memory.

Such an excess of emotion. It was unseemly.

"That was good of you, Hetty." Creasy jumped in at the opportunity. "But let me tell you my own information."

I decided to humor him.

"There is a witness to Rufus Catesby quarreling with the dancing master in public. It appears that Catesby owed Perkney a goodly sum of money, and Catesby has the devil's own temper." Creasy frowned. He had reason to know about Catesby's temper. "We must add Rufus Catesby to our list. He is a far better suspect than the poor lady."

"We seem to have uncovered a veritable Noah's Arc of suspects, then. And I can't see Mary Ellicott harming her precious dancing master. I don't think she killed him, Creasy, but I wouldn't put it past her husband. You'll have to look into his whereabouts. Have you spoken to Major Carp yet?" I paused. Creasy gave a negative nod and began to speak. I only half-listened as I gathered my own thoughts. What was I to do with Betsy Binning's love letters?

After Mary Ellicott's histrionics I'd expected Betsy Binning to remain in control of her emotions. Perhaps some sniffles, or a furtive wipe of her blue eyes, but in all an acceptance of God's will. Mistress Binning lives a well-ordered life in a well-ordered house. She well-orderly ordered me out of her house before I'd a chance to speak. All I did was walk into her well-ordered parlor. Betsy gave me one look and announced that she did not want to speak to me and I should leave her house upon the instant. She even rang the bell for the maid-servant who had shown me in. I'd hoped to extend my sympathy upon her loss and here I was shown to the door. I'd no chance to return the letters she'd written to the dancing master. I couldn't in conscience turn them over to the maid, for fear other eyes than Betsy's might peruse them.

I caught some words as Creasy spoke, something about a fight, and a debt. But it wasn't until the words: M'sieur Germaine and supper pierced my consciousness that I pulled myself together and paid attention. One did not ignore an invitation to dine with the Huguenot merchant, who was known for the elegance and generosity of his table. I rose at once from my tavern seat. A lady's dress took time and thought upon such an occasion.

TEN

Our smiling host greeted Creasy and me with an outstretched arm, the wrist dripping with elegant lace. "Only an informal supper, my friends. Just a quiet evening with a little dancing afterwards, for those who choose to join in."

The hall was ablaze with light from candelabras placed judiciously in every corner and every alcove. Candles in sconces festooned the length of the walls and tin lamps shone in every window nook. People in silks, velvets and brocades milled about in a buzz of conversation and a soft rustling of fabric. Servants in livery slipped through the crowds, offering up trays filled with sugared confections and goblets of wine.

Creasy gave me a dazed look. "So much for an informal gathering," he murmured, bending to my ear. He looked respectable in his black coat and the tobacco colored waistcoat, which I'd presented to him as a gift for the occasion. Such a dinner called for proper dress, and I was determined that a Boston minister should do the town credit. The waistcoat was of ribbed silk with silver gilt buttons, simple and dignified but of the best quality.

For myself I'd commissioned a robe of dusky rose color with a pink silk ruched petticoat, plain, as my robe was of scallop-pattern brocade. I wore a small bouquet of posies in my hair and one at my bodice. Filmy antique lace flowed from my sleeves. I looked very well in my dress, and when one feels confident that one looks one's best, that confidence shows in one's bearing. I needed all the confidence I could muster when I met my dinner partner.

I nodded to M'sieur, a giddy sensation filling my head. I do love a convivial evening, and this one looked to be convivial in the extreme. M'sieur placed an arm around both our shoulders and bore us towards the masses.

"These English ladies of whom you spoke have returned to England, so I've asked two people to partner you at supper tonight. I hope that's not too forward of me. I wasn't sure whether you are acquainted with the people here, and the duties of a host. Well, you know how busy they keep one." He squeezed my shoulder.

Did he not think we of the Bay Colony knew how to enjoy ourselves? We give parties and balls upon many occasions. I minded my manners, however, and did not say a word. M'sieur led me to a tall, handsome-looking gentleman who stood beside a brocade-covered chair. In the chair sat a dark-haired, bold-eyed woman whose predatory gleam shone upon Creasy with the avarice of a hawk spotting a mouse in the grass.

The tall gentleman bowed over my hand, saluting my fingers with dry, warm and charming lips. I liked his face, a high-bridged nose, shortened upper lip, amused gray eyes, long, smooth-shaven chin, his unpowdered hair the color of polished chestnut. He held my hand within his long fingers a fraction longer than necessary as he gazed down upon me, waiting for the introduction.

I heard my host say my name and caught the gentleman's name as, "My cousin Alexandre Bernon." My knees felt like warm pudding. The buzz in my ears was not from the crowd, I realized. I pulled myself together in time to accept his arm and to follow him to the ends of the earth, which turned out to be the supper table. The slight pressure of his hand upon my arm as he relinquished it to draw out my chair, melted my limbs so that I fell into the seat with a clumsy plop. The hint of a grin creased the long mouth.

Come, I scolded myself, you've seen fine-looking gentlemen before. But not one so tall, with such broad shoulders in that fitted blue coat, with such powerful thighs in those tight breeches and well-shaped legs in those white stockings. And this Adonis was to be mine for the evening. Crystal glassware sparkled upon crisp white linens, the branched candelabra ablaze in the table center, and this gentleman to be my companion. Ah, how wondrous the evening ahead. Don't spoil it, I warned myself, by acting like a goose.

Fortunately for me, the gentleman proved as capable in thought and speech as he was comely in his person, so that my awkward laughs and sprightly head tosses went unnoticed by the rest of the table. No matter how much I reprimanded myself for my silly behavior, I continually lost myself in those gray eyes that sparkled with hidden laughter, or the long mouth with the sweet curve that I imagined pressing upon mine. Even a simple courtesy like his saying that he looked forward to making my acquaintance, and I felt as giddy as if I'd drunk eight glasses of Rhenish wine—which I may have done, so far as I was aware. At his statement that M'sieur sang my praises, I simpered like a green girl. Finally I was forced to pinch my wrist beneath the tablecloth so that I could form a polite answer. He's only a man, I told myself, but what a man. I promptly shivered with delight, warning myself not to giggle, please Lord, not to giggle.

"Oh, I was prepared to believe in your ability to command a fleet of merchant ships," the gentleman said. "I know that women are quite capable of such feats—but I confess to reservations when M'sieur said you were a lovely as you are able."

The gentleman went on in such a manner that I had to fan myself to keep my blushes from overwhelming my features.

"How dared I doubt my good friend's judgment," he said, those long lips opening in a smile.

The gentleman leaned in towards me and I became very aware of the broad shoulders beneath the fine tailoring of a dark blue coat. I gave myself a mental reprimand for my foolish giggle. What was wrong with me? I don't usually act like such a goose, but my mind was wrapped in a woolen fleece. I eyed the long-stemmed goblet of wine I'd been sipping and vowed to lift the glass no longer.

"My cousin Germaine did not do you justice, Madame." Alexandre spoke in a low, intimate tone. "Words like *hair the color of honey* and *eyes like jade stones* do not convey the beauty of its subject. No, mere words cannot capture the spirit and warmth of such a lovely woman."

I hoped with fervor that my companion could not feel my inner warmth, lest he be burned to an ash. "Sir," I said, finding my voice—it was a little high-pitched, but it was my voice. "You flatter me. We are taught that modesty is the greater virtue, all else is vanity."

"Ah, but honesty compels me to speak, Madame. Is not honesty the greater of the virtues?" His smile revealed good, even teeth.

"Modesty prevails, Sir, even above honesty. At least in such situations as this, in civil discourse." That was my answer.

"Well then, Mrs. Henry, if I am not allowed to praise your beauty, we shall have to change the direction of our conversation."

I gave a brief nod of agreement.

"For instance, I very much admire your dress. You look like a garden of beautiful roses." He touched his hand lightly to his heart. "Soon enough there will be fields of roses that herald your arrival. At least, that is what I will think when I see them. And that web of lace at your sleeve—as delicate as the morning dew."

I was proud of the costly lace that adorned my gown. I appreciated his notice, but I thought his praise rather fulsome than warranted. Creasy, who sat opposite me at the table, had not noticed my gown or my laces. If he had, he would have questioned the extravagance of both. Although he had accepted my gift of the silk vest with an unaccustomed grace.

Creasy was seated between the bold dark woman and a fair, mousy lady. The table held ten to a side, with our host presiding at the head and an elderly woman, his aunt, at the foot. My partner to the left was a rotund Boston merchant, Tobias Cox, whom I knew from commerce. We chatted for a moment between the soup course and the fish course, which was a delicious sole poached in white wine. The platters of fish were followed by the meat course, a loin of veal with caper sauce and a ragout of venison. I noted with pleasure that my companion, Alexandre Bernon, ate with a hearty appetite. I mistrust gentlemen who fidget with their food.

Over bowls of sugared confits, raisins and nuts, my handsome gentleman and I resumed our conversation. "You are a connoisseur of woman's clothing, Sir. How did you learn so much about ladies' finery? Are you one of those charming gentlemen who scour the shops for the latest fashions to procure for your wife?"

Alexandre shook his head. "I have an eye for a pretty woman, that is all. As for a wife, alas, I am a widower. She died in London three years ago. The shock of leaving our homeland, of fleeing for our lives, in truth, and the terrible English weather... Well, she could not survive the ordeal."

"Oh, I am sorry." I meant it.

"It is as the Lord wills." He shrugged a broad shoulder. "Did not your grandfathers experience the hardships of leaving one homeland for another? Were not the conditions even more perilous? This city of Boston is a prosperous place, but a day's ride from here and one is in wilderness. We Huguenots did not have to face the barbarous painted savages...only the English."

I felt a pang of annoyance at his words. A certain native of the Northern woods came to mind, one who was as much a gentleman as my current companion, even if he did sometimes paint his face and knock his enemies on the head with a deadly club. At least once that *savage* had saved my life. Twice, if I counted the time I'd dealt with a pirate while Blue Bear's fierce aspect kept the pirate from making unwelcome overtures.

From curiosity, I asked if he had been north to the Albany colony. "There is the real wilderness, where the pines tower over the land and no sunlight penetrates their boughs," I said, nearly able to smell the spicy scent of fir and balsam.

"I think I prefer Boston and the sea, thank you." The gentleman's gray eyes sparkled.

Beneath the tailored coat of dark blue he wore a buff-colored waistcoat embroidered with silken threads of blue, green and gold. The lace that fell in folds from his neck and his cuffs was quite as fine as my own.

"How long will you grace us with your presence here?" I hoped for a very long time.

"One night," he said.

My face must have shown my disappointment.

"I shall impose upon M'sieur Germaine for tonight but tomorrow I move into my own quarters. Who knows how long I shall remain in Boston? I find the citizens of your town utterly charming." The gentleman smiled.

He shifted his position slightly so that I felt his broad shoulder touching mine. My limbs grew numb. I could not have risen from my chair had they shouted "Fire!" into my ears. It was just as well that the merchant upon my left, Tobias Cox, claimed my attention at that moment, his pudgy hand tugging at my sleeve. I was glad to give him what attention I was capable of giving, as I needed time to regain my composure.

Mr. Cox caught the word 'commerce' and wished to consult me upon a certain property he thought to acquire, and did I think the price too high? I encouraged him to relate the merits of the site and its drawback. We agreed that, with the drainage of a parcel of marsh, he would gain possession of an agreeable property.

"If you do not benefit from it directly, your heirs shall," I said.

"But I have no heirs. At least only a cousin, and he is a great clod. I should not like him to benefit from it at all." The gentleman's face flushed bright scarlet.

As I had no reply to his objections, I turned toward my Huguenot companion and found him in conversation with the woman at his right hand. I suffered a brief pang of jealousy, but the woman was stout, pockmarked and happily married. Although I'd just witnessed the effects of a charming scoundrel like Francis Perkney upon married women. Across the table, Creasy sat deep in conversation with the bold-eyed hawk while the fair-haired mouse gazed adoringly at him. I wagered to myself that the dark woman would carry off with the spoils. Creasy did not know how to deny a strong-minded woman. I do not mean this as an affront, I have found it a handy attribute, myself.

I fingered the long, green stem of my goblet until my handsome Alexandre turned back to me, raising his glass to my health. As it became clear that the supper was concluded, he stood up, leaning over as he pulled out my chair.

"Do you remain for the dancing?" he asked.

"No," I said, feeling some regret. "I may not."

"May I see you home?"

I glanced over at Creasy, who was still seated, speaking to an enthralled mousy woman. The dark-haired woman had risen from her chair and taken her leave. I shook my head. "I have an escort. Mister Cotton brought me. He will see me home... But I thank you for the offer."

"Then allow me to help you with your cloak." He took my arm, leading me by a circuitous route in a tour of the first floor of the grand house until we finally reached the hall where servants waited with cloaks over their arms. I felt a tinge of disappointment the tour had ended.

I pointed out my blue velvet cloak with its white ermine trim and Alexandre draped it around my shoulders.

"Very pretty," he said. "Very pretty indeed."

"The cloak is a present from an acquaintance." I pulled the cloak about me. I'd won it in a wager with a pirate, but I was not about to reveal its provenance.

"Oh, yes. The cloak is pretty too," Alexandre murmured. His lips brushed my ear as he spoke. "Will you take a little supper with me tomorrow evening?"

I nodded, not trusting my voice. My knees threatened to melt beneath me.

"I shall come for you at five o'clock," he said.

Alexandre's words purred in my ear all the way home. Had Creasy not been so enthralled in singing the praises of his two dinner companions he might have noticed my unusual silence. I fostered his talk, content in my own reflections. "Did you enjoy your companions?" I asked.

"I did, but not quite as much as you enjoyed yours."

So he had noticed. I hurried on, hoping to lure him away from that topic. "You seemed to give your attention to the dark-haired lady. Was she so very agreeable?"

"My companion was most agreeable. Had you been paying attention I should have introduced you to her. But perhaps you know her? She is Eliza Welsteed, sister by marriage to one of our suspects. I believe you questioned Sarah Welsteed, did you not?"

"I did," I said, "but she is not one of our suspects. Her son broke his leg and she was there to care for him at the time Perkney was murdered. I have not had the pleasure of meeting Miss Welsteed. She has been living in New Hampshire, I believe, until called to come help care for her nephew."

Creasy nodded in agreement. "Miss Welsteed mentioned her nephew's accident. She did not like to leave the little fellow for M'sieur's dinner. She only came at the insistence of her sister-in-law, and she felt compelled to leave early to help with the boy. Miss Welsteed was kind enough to say she was glad she had come because it gave her the opportunity to make my acquaintance."

I noted Creasy's self-satisfied smirk but I chose to ignore it. I was in a forgiving mood. For the remainder of our walk we kept our own thoughts. At the warehouse door I took a quick leave of him only to call him back in a voice that squeaked.

ELEVEN

I knew something was wrong as soon as I lifted the latch and the door opened. It should have been barred from within. I ran back out into the street, calling out for Creasy but trying to modulate my cries. If a robber was inside, I did not want to alert him. We might be able to capture him if taken unawares.

Creasy heard me and turned back at once. "What's wrong?"

"I'm not sure, but the door is unlatched. It shouldn't be. Where's my watchman? I don't like it, Creasy. I don't like it at all." I turned back to the door of the warehouse.

Creasy grabbed my arm, halting me. "Wait. We should call for the Watch."

I knew Creasy was no coward and I knew this was a sensible suggestion, but I felt too impatient to wait for the doddering old man who acted as Town Watch. "Go call him," I said. "I'm going inside."

Creasy kept his grip upon me so that I could not turn. "At least he has a staff, Hetty. We don't have a weapon. There's been murder done not far from here. We can't take any chances."

While his argument registered in my brain, I felt I could not hesitate. I had my own man hired to watch the warehouse and my rooms upstairs. Where was he? He should have made himself known by now. Perhaps he lay inside, injured—murdered—I had to know. "I'm going inside." I jerked my arm free.

Creasy muttered under his breath but he followed me inside. I stepped into a room black as pitch and paused to adjust my eyes. Creasy stepped upon my heel. I yelped.

"Sorry." His whisper barely caught my ears.

I turned, my face so close to his I felt his breath. "Get the torch from outside the door." I gave him a push. There should have been torches lit by the inside door, and candles to light the staircase to my rooms. We could not proceed without light, yet the torch would most certainly give away our presence. It could not be helped, however.

I breathed a sigh of relief when Creasy reappeared with the torch. Its light revealed that the boxes and bales were still in neat rows, as I'd left them. I called for the watchman.

"Samuel. Samuel Goodsell! Where are you?" An icy stream filled my veins at the silence. Of course Samuel was an old man, he could be ill, he could be asleep, although he was not paid to sleep and should receive a blistering scold from me if that proved to be the case. I moved forward at a rapid pace. I heard Creasy bump into a box behind me. The office door opened at my touch; I pushed it and paused.

Creasy swept past me, the torch illuminating a floor littered with papers, ledgers and overturned boxes. I gasped. The icy waters of my blood steamed up like a volcano. If there is anything I detest, it's an untidy office.

A lump beneath the papers stirred and groaned. "Samuel." I could not help but cry out the poor man's name.

We rushed forward to uncover the good old man, tied and gagged like an old scold on a ducking stool. Creasy held the torch while I produced a small knife from my pocket and cut away at the ropes that bound him. The old man himself removed the cloth that covered his mouth. The curses that sprung from that mouth did more to reassure me that my watchman was unharmed than the movement of his limbs. He sat up, rubbing his head.

"I was hit from behind by those snakes," he said. "I come to and couldn't move. I'm that sorry, Mrs. Henry. I never heard 'em comin'."

"Let me look at your head." It was a command, not a request.

"Let's see if you're hurt."

"Me head is as hard as an anvil," Samuel said. He ducked away from my hand. "Don't you worry about that. It'll take more than a knock to break this ol' noggin."

The old man would have stood up but I held him down with my hands upon his shoulders. "Creasy, go across the street and shout out for my neighbor. You know Adam Hull. Ask him to fetch the constable."

Creasy straightened to do my bidding, but then he paused. "I don't like to leave you alone."

"We'll be fine. I've got Samuel here with me. He's not likely to be caught unawares again." My words were meant to hearten the old man.

"Where's my club?" Samuel looked around. "They'll not get me this time, Mrs. Henry."

I nodded at Creasy, who took himself off. A blast of cold air reached us from the open door. I heard Creasy yelling loud enough to wake the dead, then he was back at my side. In moments a crowd of people filed through the door, many of them in night robes and caps. Samuel became the center of attention. Gesturing Creasy to follow, I dashed up the steps to my rooms. Had the intruders broken into my private quarters? The thought that my clean floors might be strewn with papers and broken pottery made my guts roil. With a sigh of relief I saw that my rooms were neat and tidy, as I'd left them for M'sieur's supper gathering. I closed my door and went back down to thank my neighbors for their help and concern. By then the constable had arrived.

Phillymort seemed to believe that old Samuel had hit himself on the head and tied himself up, but I ignored his jibes. I insisted he escort old Samuel back to his home and pushed him out the door, poor Samuel following. "I'll send a physician to you, Samuel," I said, ignoring his protests that he did not need a doctor. I gestured to my neighbor, Mister Hull, who lingered by the doorway in case he was needed. Hull, a hearty man in his fifties, took himself off to run for the physician.

Samuel's care seen to, I sank into my desk chair. "I'll have to go through every piece of paper in every ledger." I waved my hand at the chaos upon the floor.

"You don't have to do it tonight," Creasy said. "I'll stay down here while you sleep… I know you'll worry about it if someone's not on watch."

He was right about that, I would worry. Still, I couldn't let him sit up all night on my behalf. I decided to be sensible. "No," I said. "You go home. I'll lock up after you and start to clean up in the morning. I promise." With an effort I rose from the chair to follow my own instructions. I plodded up the stairs to my room and my bed, where I fell into a deep sleep.

I needed that sleep for the job I faced in the morning. Invoices and bills of lading must be crosschecked against ledger entries… page after page of ledger entries. While my clerk could help me to some extent, I would not put the whole business upon his shoulders. It was my carelessness that caused the mess. Samuel was simply too old a guard.

～

Creasy pulled tight his cape and lowered his head against the chill of the wind. It was after the witching hour and he longed for his bed. What a strange night. First the pleasure of dining with M'sieur Germaine, with good food, abundant wine, and Hetty in such a good mood. Then the awful scare at her warehouse. Poor Samuel Goodsell. Seeing the old man on the floor like that—-he'd thought there's been another murder. Hetty thought the same. He'd felt how tense were the muscles in her arm, even through her velvet cloak. What ever possessed her to wear a velvet cloak like that? Too light by far for March weather. Showing off for M'sieur and his company, no doubt. The vanity of a woman. Well, she was a woman, come to that, and a very willful woman. He hadn't wanted to leave her. After all, her office had been ransacked. Hetty insisted she'd be safe, and you couldn't argue with her when she got into one of her moods. The truth was, Hetty Henry could deal with any rogue, and then some.

Creasy's steps quickened as he approached his Summer Street house. The little building was almost hidden by the church in the black night. The house wasn't much: a parlor, a tiny kitchen with a hearth, a study and a bedroom at the top of the narrow staircase. It suited Creasy to live in small surroundings, as he had no wife and a poor congregation of sailors, widows and laborers. His church could barely afford to keep him in firewood; therefore, he took pains to bank his fire before leaving his abode. The darkness that greeted him upon his doorstep came as no surprise. He stepped into his parlor, fumbling in the dark for the peg upon which he hung his cloak. The chill that seeped through coat and waistcoat made him shiver. For a moment he did wish for a blazing hearth, but the knowledge that his bed awaited him with its goose down coverlet consoled him. The sooner he jumped under that coverlet the better, he thought, and turned to go up the staircase to its haven.

A flicker of light caught the corner of his eye. Was that a light coming from his study door? Had he failed to properly bank the hearth there? The threat of fire spreading through his little house caused his guts to twist in knots. Fire was always a fear in Boston, where the houses were close together. Leather fire buckets were kept near the front doors for handy use as neighbors all pitched in for the fight. Bucket brigades were swiftly formed to the nearest pond.

In three strides Creasy crossed the room to the study door, which was open a crack. He usually closed the door to conserve heat in the room. It's where he spent most of his time preparing and writing his sermons. Creasy flung open the door, stepping into a darkened room. He could see no sign of a spark from the hearth. The blow to his head dropped him like a hot nail on an anvil.

TWELVE

Next morning I dressed in a plain smock and petticoat, forcing myself to hours of checking invoices against ledger figures. Not long after I'd begun my drudgery, I received a note from Creasy saying he had been attacked last night but he'd suffered nothing worse than a bump on the head. I was not to worry about him but I was to keep up my own guard. He speculated that the intruder might have been looking for the ledger. *I can think of no other possible reason for the man to commit such an attack upon a minister of the Lord.* I read his outrage in the stiffened, straight letters from his pen.

I wrote a swift reply, apologizing for not rushing to his side, but if he needed me he must send back the messenger with word and I would come immediately. Would he care to join me with M'sieur for supper at five o'clock? He would be most welcome, I wrote, failing to specify that I was meeting Alexandre Bernon, and not Creasy's friend Gabriel. I penned a second brief message and sent a boy off to deliver both missives. I felt a bit of guilt for not going to Creasy to commiserate with him in person, he had been attacked in his own parsonage, after all. Who would do such a thing? I was very much afraid the villain who had attacked old Samuel had turned upon my friend. Was this the same person who murdered poor Perkney? I felt obligated to protect Creasy from further harm, for I had the means and he had not.

Less than an hour later my missive bore fruit. Before me stood the Ferret, an old, shiny and worn castor hat in his hand, an oversized coat encasing his thin body. The Ferret was a useful spy now grown into a young man of fifteen or so years. By his side stood his twin, a feminine version with the same sharp nose, beady eyes, narrow chin and thin mouth softened into an elfin grace. A Ferretina, I gathered, looking at the small being with some curiosity.

"This is Maria, my sister." The Ferret made this introduction with a gentlemanly bow.

The young maid attempted to copy this bow but the Ferret jerked her arm, forcing her upright. "A lady don't bow, you goose, she curtsies."

Maria's cheeks reddened. She gave her brother a dagger look.

"I had to bring her, Hetty." The Ferret went on. "She ain't safe where she is. She's real good at needlework. I thought maybe you could use her. Give her a torn cloth and she'll sew it right up, good's new. Go ahead," he said, pointing at me. "Get her something to sew while we talk. You'll see how good she does."

I obliged the boy, going to my sewing pile and pulling out the first thing I found, which was a handkerchief with torn lace. I had quite a pile grown, as sewing was not one of my skills. The girl produced needle and thread from her apron and took a seat by the window.

The Ferret and I seated ourselves at the hearth table. He leaned across, speaking in a confidential tone, "I'm glad you sent for me, Hetty. I was at my wit's end. It's Mum's gentlemen, you see. Some of 'em are starting to notice Maria. Well, one gave her a some words, and I ain't around to protect her all the time, me being Mr. Kegleigh's clerk and all."

In actual fact, the Ferret was more of a messenger boy, but at least he had a job. His unfortunate mother supported the rest of her brood by reclining upon her back. I did not judge. Looking at the girl I could sympathize with her predicament. She must be slightly older than the Ferret—by nine months, perhaps, but not by years.

"You say she's good with the needle?" I stalled for more time to consider the sister.

"You'll see. She's a good seamstress. I was hoping you could find a place for her. You allus look so…so very neat, and you a busy-ness woman. Why, I expect you are the busy-nesst woman I ever met." The Ferret shook his shaggy head.

"How old is Ferr… I mean, Maria, is it?" I'd nearly said *Ferretina*.

"She's sixteen, and she's a good girl, Hetty. She won't give you no trouble. She does as she's bid, our Maria. As a fact, that's why I brung her here."

"Well…" I said, considering. "I do have quite a pile of mending that needs to be done. Let's see how she's getting along on that handkerchief. If I find it to my liking she can work for me. I may recommend her to my seamstress for steady work."

"Thank you, Hetty, thank you. I been that worried about her. Now, what can I do for you?"

I liked that the boy got right to the point. "I want you to keep an eye on Mister Cotton for me. Mister Increase Cotton, that is."

"I get to spy for you again?" The boy's face lit up. "How 'bout Celia? Is she goin' to spy with me? She's good at it."

In the not distant past I had asked the two children to 'spy' for me, mainly to keep them out of trouble. Celia Edwards had come into a comfortable estate since then, and I was certain her aunt would be dismayed at the thought of her charge stooping so low. "No, no. It's nothing like that," I said, speaking quickly. "I don't want you to spy on Creasy—Mister Cotton—I just want you to keep near him without him knowing." At the Ferret's raised eyebrows I went on to explain. "I want you to protect him from harm. Just raise a ruckus if you see anyone try to hurt him You know, cry out as loud as you can. Mister Cotton was hit on the head last night. Follow him around in case the villain tries again."

The Ferret's beady eyes gleamed. "You're doin' another murder, that's what. Who is it? Not out our way this time. I got it.

The fencin' man, that's who it's got to be. Oh, wait'll Celia hears about this."

"I don't want Celia brought into this, Fer... Eliphalet." I spoke in a stern voice. The child was bright as a button but she was only a child, younger than the Ferret.

"Yes Ma'am." The boy answered a bit too quickly.

But I knew the Ferret was as good as his name. We came to terms and I wrote a note to Mister Kegleigh, Ferret's employer, that I would need his services for the next few weeks. Harry Kegleigh owed me a favor. As I handed the boy an advance upon his expenses, my attention was claimed by his sister, who rose from her chair and handed me her piece of linen. The tear in the lace was no longer visible and the corner of linen was embroidered with a white rose in silk thread. It was really quite lovely.

"Can you do this rose on my sheets and pillow covers?" I asked, a sudden vision of the most exquisite bed linens in the town filling my head. How the good wives of Boston, who slavishly copied the latest fashions of London and Paris, would envy me. My own needle skills were limited to repairing coarse sails for my ships, and then only when a hurricane struck, shredded the sails, and I had no other option but to sew or to let my boat drift like a cork.

The girl nodded, her dark curls bobbing energetically.

"Good. Then you'll stay here with me. When my mending is done and the linens embroidered, I'll ask my dressmaker to employ you." I named a wage. "Will that suit?"

The dark curls bobbed in agreement. I noticed with approval that the girl went unbidden to her chair and dipped into the sewing basket. I returned to my own work.

I came to a start when I realized it was past the dinner hour and time to array myself for the approaching supper with my gallant Huguenot cavalier. I slammed shut the ledger in which I had entered figures, left it upon my desk and ran up the stairs to my private apartments. Once inside I made an onslaught upon two chests, pulling out neatly folded robes, petticoats and shawls, holding up each one and discarding them in a heap upon the floor behind me. Whatever should I wear? I finally decided upon a plain peach robe with full lace collar, the lace of good quality but not extravagant. It exposed the slope of my shoulders and hinted at my bosoms. I knew I possessed good bosoms.

I turned when the Ferretina clapped her hands in approval. She stood behind me, eyeing the clothes I'd discarded. She swooped, pulled loose a shawl of sand-color from the pile, and draped it around my shoulders in a careless effect. I looked in the mirror and nodded. She then tugged at the ribbon that held back my hair and let it loose. In a quick motion she twisted strands around her finger and coaxed them into quite becoming curls. I had to admit that I looked very *a la mode*. The Ferretina was proving useful indeed.

My cavalier's reaction to my appearance left nothing to be desired. The gray eyes sparkled and the long mouth creased in a smile. Alexandre took my hand, bent and kissed it. His arm slipped around my waist as he led me to the coach. Both hands lifted me up to the first step as easily as if I'd been a bouquet of flowers. I climbed into the coach, he following.

"Where are we going?" I asked. I settled back against the cushions.

"A countryman of mine keeps a tavern in Roxbury. He serves an excellent meal. I think you'll approve."

"I'm sure I shall."

He spoke of interesting topics, telling me something of his history, the plight of the Huguenots forced to flee France for their lives, and of the kindness the people of Rhode Island showed to him. I revised my mental opinion of the colony that Cousin Cotton Mather referred to as 'Rogue Island.' I would no longer be able to laugh at such a reference.

When he dropped his effusive compliments, Alexandre Bernon proved a charming companion. I was fully aware of his physical presence. He wore a black coat with a dark red embroidered vest with gray knee breeches and white stockings displaying powerful thighs and a graceful leg. I was determined to proceed with caution, and to overcome the natural attraction he held for me. Fortunately the ease of his conversation enchanted me so that my attention was diverted somewhat from his physical presence.

The drive to Roxbury passed in no time. Alexandre was quite correct in his estimation of the meal, which was beyond excellent. I devoured a white fish poached in wine, a kind of pudding made with chicken slices and breadcrumbs, a vegetable ragout, and finally, a plum tart with custard. I was glad to see that my companion ate as heartily as did I, for I like a man who enjoys his food. We drank a light white wine with our meal.

"Are you settled into your new residence?" I leaned back against the coach cushions for the return journey.

"Yes, and I'd like to show it to you," he said. His shoulder pressed against mine.

"I'd like to see it," I managed to say. Thank goodness I was sitting, for my legs seemed to have melted beneath me. I tried to take a deep breath without alerting my companion to the fact that I needed a deep breath.

The coach went over a bump and I was thrown against Alexandre. He put his arm around me, holding me until I pulled away, which required a real effort of will. I don't know this man, I scolded myself. It's too soon. But the truth was, I hadn't felt this way for many months. I grabbed the coach strap with both hands and hung on for dear life.

It was dark when we reached our destination. Alexandre produced a large key and unlocked the door to what appeared to be a warehouse. Well, he would need space for fencing lessons. One candle shone from a wall sconce, its light showing little more than the wall behind it.

"Henry!" Alexandre's cry echoed through the empty space.

I gave a start, a numb sensation filling me as a familiar apparition appeared from out of the dark.

"Henry, light the candles, please. I have a friend with me and I'd like to show her the studio."

"Mrs. Henry." Henry nodded to me before he took his own

light and ignited the candles until the hall was a blaze of light.

"But... But this is the place... This is the place where the murder happened."

"I know. It's most unfortunate, but I can't afford to let the space go unused. You've been here before?" Alexandre looked down at me from his very masculine height.

"Oh, yes. In connection with the murder, you understand. You do know that Creasy—that's Mister Cotton of Summer Street Church—Mister Cotton and I have been asked to look into the murder? We've had some small successes in these matters. Solving crimes, I mean." I found myself stammering. The man had such an unsettling effect upon me.

"I wish you luck, then, for it isn't good for my business to have a murder hanging over it." His tone was quite grim, his long mouth tightened into a line.

"Your business?" I looked up at the gentleman, somewhat bewildered.

"I own the building, and the dancing school. Francis Perkney ran it for me. I have my own school in Providence, you know. We teach dancing and fencing. Francis thought we should expand into Boston. We didn't anticipate the opposition from the ministers or the fines we'd have to pay to the magistrates. Still, it's a profitable pursuit." Alexandre shrugged one broad shoulder. "I'll keep it going myself until I can find someone suitable to take over."

"You'll keep it going?" I sounded like a parrot, I'm sure.

"Just until I can find someone else to run it," he said.

The man had me so confused. Alexandre ran a dancing school? He owned this building? I looked down the length of the long building with its wooden floor. But a murder had been committed here. Was he not afraid of the murderer? Could the villain strike again? Was the man safe? I regarded him with concern, which I'm certain showed in my face. What was the man thinking, to flaunt a killer?

"Did you know that Mister Cotton—Creasy—was attacked last night?"

Alexandre shook his handsome head in the negative.

"He was struck from behind in his own study. He thinks his attacker was looking for the ledger. Francis Perkney's ledger." I placed my hand upon his arm, feeling some urgency. "It's your ledger. Please be careful, Alexandre. Someone wants that book. You may be in danger."

Alexandre grinned, ignoring my concern. "Come, let me show you what I've done here." He took my hand within his and led me down the room "It's quite a good space. The location, the price makes it a bargain," he said. "Of course I hope the murderer is caught soon. If there is anything I can do to help you…" He looked down at me, his expression became serious. "I don't like the idea of you being involved in this with a killer on the loose. I could keep you safe, if you'll allow me to help." He patted the sword he wore at his side.

"Thank you," I said. "It would help if you could tell me about Francis Perkney. I didn't know him, you see. What was he like? Was he of a combative nature? Did he make enemies?"

Alexandre shook his head. "In our business it does not pay to make enemies. Even if our students get carried away with the foil and attack us, we are careful to keep a cheerful disposition."

"What about the dancing school? It seems Master Perkney was certainly cheerful with his ladies." I thought of all the women I'd interviewed. None of them complained about the service. What was there about the man? How had I missed hearing about him and his lessons? If only I'd been a lady of leisure. Drat the mercantile business. There were many men in Boston who had advised me to stay at home like a good wife, but my second husband, Mister Henry, had encouraged me to pursue my business abilities. I looked up at the tall man beside me and knew how I'd like to pass my time, should I ever have any leisure. No wonder the ladies had succumbed to Perkney if he was half as charming as his partner.

My companion's handsomely arched brows drew together. "Francis overstepped the bounds there. I warned him about becoming too familiar with his pupils. We are teachers. There must be a respect accorded to that position. We must not take advantage of the trust developed between pupil and teacher."

I was impressed by the sincerity in his voice. "Were you never tempted, yourself?" I could not help asking the question. Were I one of his pupils I'm sure I would set my cap at him.

Alexandre shrugged one of his broad shoulders. "I try to establish the proper distance from the first lesson. But then, I teach mostly fencing, not dance. Of course, if the lady by my side were to become a pupil of mine, I would not vouch for keeping such a lofty distance."

The smile he directed at me caused a tiny flame to lick at my groin. It was most uncomfortable.

Alexandre stopped at the door to Perkney's private rooms. He reached for the doorknob but I pulled loose my hand, shaking my head. The image of the large curtained bed intruded upon my thoughts. It was too soon for such intimacy between Alexandre and me. "Mister Cotton and I have seen your quarters," I said. I had to make a real effort to keep my voice from trembling. "In fact, I must confess that we searched your quarters. We found your ledger and we were going to study it, but through no fault of our own, we lost it. I'm very sorry about that. One day it was there, the next day it was gone," I faltered.

Alexandre patted my hand, which still rested upon his arm. "Don't distress yourself, my dear. I have it."

I jerked my hand away without thinking. "You? Where did you find it? We searched and searched—"

His head tilted toward me, the edges of his long mouth creased. "When I received notice of Francis' death, I rode up from Providence—I spent most of the night in the saddle. I retrieved the ledger and barely made it to my cousin's home for some sleep. It was Gabriel who sent me word. And I must make arrangements for the funeral, you know. Poor Francis had no kin."

I felt light-headed. "So—you've had the ledger all this while?"

"Yes. It's in safe keeping."

"May we see it? It may have a bearing upon Perkney's death."

"Of course, under the circumstances." He gave a slight nod. I felt like a weight had been lifted from my shoulder—the weight of a dead man. I would not care to let a stranger examine my ledgers, although I kept them in perfect order. It was bad enough having to go through those love letters... I'm sure my face grew crimson recalling the events of that day. I did not usually have feelings of gratitude for Constable Phillymort, but he had earned them then. For once his entrance was anything but ill timed.

"Shouldn't you like to see the improvements I've made? I thought Master Perkney a bit shabby in his furnishings."

Once more I thought of the great bed with the velvet hangings and the indelicate situation I'd found myself in with Creasy. I'm sure my face flushed, even as I shook my head in the negative.

Alexandre was gentleman enough to accept my denial with grace and to escort me back to the carriage. I tried to take my leave of him outside the vehicle but he insisted upon accompanying me back to my rooms above my own warehouse. He saw me safely inside with just a kiss upon my gloved hand. I thought my knees would buckle and I'd drop to the ground, but I managed to stagger inside and bolt the door. I leaned against the door while the horses drew the carriage away down the street. Drat the man and his cursed effect upon me. I scolded my foolish yearning all the way up the stairs to my bed.

THIRTEEN

Creasy watched as the militia marched across the green in neat rows, half-pikes upon their shoulders straight as a line of fence. Major Carp's company wore ordinary linen smocks and buff breeches save that a scarlet sash draped over each shoulder. Major Carp stood watching, a scarlet sash across his shoulder like his troop, except that a sword in its scabbard hung from his waist. He looked a most martial figure.

The company sergeant flung out commands while a little boy in a purple coat and gray breeches thrummed beats upon his little drum. Come Training Day the company would show well and perhaps win a medal in competition, Creasy thought. He hoped to have a word with the major after the drill so he followed the company across the green, where they were dismissed. The major led his men into the nearest tavern. Creasy lost sight of his quarry as the cheering troops overflowed the doorway forcing him to wait until the shoving was over and all the men were safely inside. He entered the tavern. The company members were crowded on benches by the wall, wiping sweaty faces and yelling out for mugs of ale. Creasy did not see the major. He squeezed himself on to the edge of a bench and beckoned to the serving woman. The young woman nodded, thrusting frothy mugs into outstretched hands as she worked her way over to Creasy's bench.

"Let's have a pitcher over here and keep it coming until these brave men have quenched their thirst."

Creasy felt his shoulder pressed with good will. "We'll be

here all night, Sir, if you order so much."

Creasy turned his head to find the company sergeant standing behind him. "I watched your company train. Very impressive. I'm sure you'll do well on Training Day." Creasy lifted his own mug and toasted the company: "To your success, Sirs."

The young serving woman returned with a tray and two large pitchers upon it. Without spilling a drop, she filled mug after mug. When one pitcher emptied, the next was employed.

Creasy turned to his neighbor. "Where is Major Carp? I thought I saw him come in with you."

The company member lowered his mug. He wiped his mouth with a sleeve. "Oh, he did. Orders a round and then takes his leave. He never drinks with us. He's a stickler for drill, is the major, but he ain't sociable. No indeed."

Creasy had hoped to catch the gentleman following a training session. Several attempts to visit at the house had come to naught. The man was never in. Where did the elusive major go? It was frustrating, and sure to become more so when he tried to explain to Hetty. 'Oh, well, I'm here. I might as well enjoy the company of this genial group,' he thought.

Several hours later, Creasy left the tavern feeling in good cheer—very good cheer. It would have been as inhospitable to refuse to drink with such fine fellows. How could he offend the men who were training to defend the good citizens of Boston? After all, he was a citizen himself. Surely sharing a glass of two was his duty, and toasting the company's military skills the least he could do to honor them. Several of the major's company had expressed a desire to hear him preach of a Sunday. Why, it might even lead to new converts to the church. The means was nothing, the outcome all. He tripped over a stone in the road and hiccoughed his apologies to a lady crossing the street, although she was in no danger of being jostled.

"Mister Cotton."

The call brought him up short, so short he wavered backward and strained to right himself. He turned his head to spot a young woman running toward him. By squinting his eyes and concentrating upon her cap and apron, he recognized the tavern girl with the tray who had supplied them with so many cups of ale. What need had she of him? Had he forgotten something? He pressed his hands to his coat pockets but nothing was missing. He was sure they had paid the bill. The young woman ran up, pressed a note into his hand and took off again to the tavern. She spoke not one word more. He placed the note in his pocket and paced sedately across the common. Time to consider the note in private, besides his head pounded furiously.

With relief and a deeply felt thanks to the ladies of his congregation he found a bowl of warm chowder set out for him. He sat at the table which he used both as desk and for dining, savoring the milky broth with chunks of potato and soft clams. There was a plate of golden johnnycake to add to the feast. The ladies often provided him with such treats, this being a custom adopted from the wealthier women of Cousin Cotton's church. Creasy appreciated his gifts all the more as his own congregation of poor widows, sailors and peddler's wives had such meager resources. But what they had they shared with him. His meal finished, he stood up and sought the sanctuary of his small study.

Creasy added a log to the fire and sat next to the hearth for a brief respite, which turned into a comforting nap. Awaking with a start when the blackened log shifted in the hearth, he reached into his coat pocket and pulled out the note forgotten there. Now, what did the wench want from him? He'd never seen her before, to his knowledge. She looked none too tidy, with strands of pale blond hair sticking out of her cap, spots on her striped apron and a bedraggled hem to her skirts. He opened the paper and read a brief message.

Mister Cotton

Sir, meet me behind the tavern at midnight tonight. I have information.

Y'er Servant, Pamela Charlotte.

The words were scrawled across the paper in a childish hand.

His inclination was to ignore the message. Why should he arise from his bed at midnight to meet a tavern girl? What sort of information could she possibly have to interest him? But then he revised his opinion. A tavern server might well overhear tidbits of information, and it was well known that he and Hetty were looking into the murder of the dancing master. And the dancing master was a womanizer and the tavern wench was a woman, for all the dirty spots upon her apron. Perhaps she knew Perkney, perhaps she had served him in the tavern. That would be most likely. Perhaps she was one of his conquests, although she certainly did not come up to the standards he'd shown in his other conquests. Charlotte... he knew of no family of that name, not in his congregation. Should he ask Hetty? Hetty Henry knew everyone of high and low stature in Boston. On the other hand, she'd insist upon coming with him to the meeting, and he had the feeling the tavern wench would not like that. There was really no need to keep Hetty from a good night's sleep. He felt a slight sense of elation that he might well uncover a piece of information that Hetty did not have. Of course, he'd share it with her, but let him savor the knowledge that he knew something Hetty Henry did not know.

Creasy crossed the common in a night as black as coal. No candles shone in the windows; the torches had been doused. Only the watches with their lanterns would penetrate this gloom. Creasy had no wish to be stopped by the watch. He listened for calls but his own shuffling boots were the only sounds to break the silence. He reached the tavern at midnight. He could hear the bongs of the tavern clock. Light from a lamp shone dim in the front window. He marched around to the back of the building where no candle gave even a hint of light. The building seemed to loom over him as black as tar. Creasy carried no lantern. He held out his hands like a blind man, which in effect, he was.

"Miss Charlotte?" He spoke in a loud whisper. "Miss Charlotte?" He was not early, he'd timed it for a precise arrival. Perhaps she'd been delayed. Well, he would wait no more than five minutes for the young lady. Five minutes and no more. Not even if she were the Queen. He took careful steps forward. Imagine arousing a servant of the Lord out of a sound sleep to keep a suspicious rendezvous. Would she play him a prank? He'd not have it. He took another step and stumbled over something, extending his hands as he caught his balance. A mound of dirt? A log? He, being a trifle nearsighted, lowered himself to his knees to examine the object. Something sticky clung to his fingers. He breathed in a sour smell. He felt cloth and cold flesh.

Creasy let out his breath in a long whoosh. He coughed twice. Finally he managed to inhale, and with the intake of air he shouted out in a voice loud enough to reach the sleeping sinners in the back pews.

"Ho. Help. Murder!"

Pamela Charlotte lay at his feet in a pool of blood. At least he thought it must be her. As his eyes adjusted to the dark he could make out her arms, thrust out like the cross of Christ. He touched her pale face, the eyes stared sightless into the dark night. Poor thing. She should have light for her journey and his prayers for her soul, but first he must get help. All good peoples were asleep in their beds at this time of night. He must awaken the tavern keeper and send for the constable. Creasy took off across the grass, heedless of the dark. He found his way to the sweet glimmer of lantern light inside the tavern and pounded upon the door. "Ho. Help. Murder!"

No one seemed to hear him. He pounded with both fists upon the thick oak. It seemed like hours before he heard the bar lifted and a voice grumbling behind it.

"Steady on… Steady on…"

Finally the thick door opened a crack and the tavern keeper poked a night-capped head around it. He lifted a candle, squinting his eyes at the young minister. "Who is it?"

Creasy blessed the candled, it's feeble gleam the only symbol of hope he could find in this night. "It's murder, Mister Cody. Murder's been done on your land. There's a body behind your tavern. Best send for the constable, please Sir."

The candle stayed steady in its position, the eyes squinted harder. "Who is it?" The taverner's voice rose in suspicion.

"It's me, Mister Cody. It's Increase Cotton of Summer Street church. I say again, please send for the constable. There's murder been done here."

The candle lifted high, the door opened a foot more and the nightcap swung this way and that. "I don't see no murder." The tavern keeper grumbled, gray brows drawn together.

"In the back, Mister Cody, behind the tavern. There's a dead body there. Please send for the constable at once." Creasy felt tears of frustration welling in his eyes. Why would this man doubt his word?

"Mayhap it's an inebriate, Sir, as is lying drunk back there. It happens, Sir, even though I will not serve a man when he's in his cups. I cut them off, Sir, but they will obtain it any way they can, and they have clever ways, Sir, clever ways. Why, you wouldn't credit it." The tavern keeper shook his head, the nightcap tassel swinging this way and that.

Creasy gestured with a crooked finger. "Come, Sir, come. See for yourself. It's not a man, it's a woman. It's the woman who serves here, and she's not inebriated, she's dead."

"Pammie?" The tavern keeper fumbled with the ties of his banyan, pulling it tight around him. "Pammie dead? I don't believe it." But he opened the door and stepped out to follow, the candle flickering wildly as he moved. Creasy strode around the building but he stopped to wait for the taverner, who shuffled along in slippers.

The light of the candle shone softly on the white mask of Pamela Charlotte's face. Wisps of pale blonde hair stuck out from beneath a lace cap. The mild blue eyes stared up sightless. A light cape lay open, revealing a robe of seafoam green, cut low to expose the lady's small bosoms, a strip of filmy lace barely serving as a modesty piece. Blood congealed around the stomach region where there appeared to be slashes in the voluminous cloth. The taverner lowered his candle to the death mask that was her face, with its twisted expression of horror. The poor woman had seen her death coming.

"That's Pammie," he said. "I'll be cursed. Begging your pardon, Sir."

Creasy nodded. "Let's carry her inside." Poor thing, to come to such a violent end. May the Lord receive her at the Gates of Heaven and judge her with mercy, he prayed. He lifted her shoulders while the taverner grabbed her legs. They staggered with the body. She was a small woman but death gave her a weight equal to a load of stone. Between them they carried her inside and laid the body upon a table. Both men fell onto the bench to catch their breaths, the taverner wiping his forehead with a piece of cloth.

"We must send for the constable." Creasy managed to gasp out his wish.

The taverner nodded, wheezing: "I'll wake my boy and send him." He bent double before he caught his breath and stood.

At his quick return both men sat upon the bench, backs turned to the body upon the table. Creasy felt he could not bear the vacant gaze of the dead woman, nor the sight of the blood-covered dress. As a minister he was used to the dead and the dying but the savage attack upon the poor woman unnerved him. He sat in silence. The taverner kept him company, and neither did that gentleman seem to feel the need for conversation. Why had the woman wanted to see him? What information had she for him? Why tell him, and not the constable? But then the constable was a hard man, perhaps she was frightened of him. Did her note even concern Perkney's murder? He'd just assumed it did. Was there anything he could have done to prevent this murder? Should he have arrived earlier? Why did he feel he had to be precise as to the time specified in the note? Perhaps he could have stayed the hand that committed this heinous crime had he not been so exact in his notions. His thoughts whirled around in his head. Mainly to stop the whirl, he turned to the taverner.

"The woman wrote me a note, saying she had information for

me. I assume it had to do with the murder of the dancing master. Did she say anything to you? Perhaps she heard something in her duties..."

The taverner only shook his head.

"Did she know Francis Perkney?" Creasy persisted. There must be some connection between the serving woman and the dancing master. If could find that connection perhaps he would find what information she had to impart. Creasy shifted his position upon the bench. The wood was hard and uncomfortable. It seemed as if the two men had sat there for hours.

The taverner thought for a moment before he spoke. He shrugged. "Pammie knew quite a few men, Sir. I can't say whether she knew that particular gentleman or not. Ah well, poor girl. She's dead now. Best not say anything ill of the dead."

The dead lay behind them on a table. Creasy felt a shiver pass over his arms. To die peacefully at home, in your own bed, was one thing. To lie in a pool of your own blood was another. She'd been stabbed savagely, many times, at close quarters. No doubt the girl knew her assailant. Creasy wished the constable would hasten. More to fill the silence, he asked of his companion: "I know you don't want to speak ill of the dead, Sir, but it may help find her killer. Was there any one man who showed a particular interest in her? Or one to whom she showed a preference?"

The taverner seemed to consider the question before he answered. "She did bring in quite a bit of custom, I must say." He paused. "But I can't say as to any preference she had for any one gentleman."

"And what kind of gentlemen would that be?" Creasy pressed the question. Pamela didn't seem the sort of woman to appeal to the men of his acquaintance, but then you never knew. Of course he'd only seen her for a brief time, and then in her work clothing. Perhaps she was more attractive when she dressed in her best. He recalled suddenly that the body behind him was dressed in good clothing, she'd worn her best for the meeting with him. He shivered involuntarily, nearly missing his companion's answer.

"Oh, all sorts, Mister Cotton. Sailors, of course. Gentlemen, too. You'd be surprised. Merchants, peddlers, some of 'em from Town here and some from away. Pammie had a way with men, you see. Me being a family man and a man of business, I knew she were good for trade, so to speak, and I didn't keep too close tabs on what she done outside of what I paid her to do. And that was to serve my customers, Sir. I'm not one to judge. I leaves that to you people, Sir." The taverner clamped shut his mouth.

Creasy felt too tired to make a response. He slumped upon the bench in silence until he heard a loud pounding upon the door. Constable Phillymort did not wait for the door to open to him, he burst his way through.

Pointing his gold-knobbed staff at Creasy the constable intoned: "'Do they not err that devise evil?' Proverbs 14-22."

"The evil devised is behind us on the table." Creasy made a brief gesture with his hand.

Constable John Phillymort advanced with a ponderous step. He frowned down at the body. "'And the nakedness of thy whoredoms shall be discovered.' Ezekial 23-29."

"She's dead," Creasy said. "Show some respect."

Phillymort narrowed his eyes, regarding Creasy. "By whose hand?" The tone was accusing.

"By the same hand who killed Francis Perkney, and it wasn't poor Joyliffe, either." The constable arrested poor Jacob Joyliffe just because he'd found the man by the body. Yet not a drop of blood was upon Joyliffe's clothing, and surely whoever skewered Master Perkney would have been splattered with blood. And poor Joyliffe was obviously in a state of shock. The man who killed Perkney—and now poor Pamela Charlotte—was cold, hard and sure of himself. Well Joyliffe couldn't be blamed for this one. Creasy would see to that.

The constable regarded him with gimlet eyes.

"I could use a cup of ale," the taverner said. He rubbed his hands.

"After hours," the constable intoned. "Not permitted."

"I'm not charging for it. My treat." The taverner headed for the wooden bar.

The constable tapped the floor with his gold-knobbed staff. "It's after hours. Not permitted."

Creasy felt the heat rise to his face.

The taverner resumed his seat. He placed a warning hand upon Creasy's shoulder. "Hadn't you better send for the coroner?" The taverner addressed the constable. "I'm sure you would like to know his findings."

"'Who is this that darkeneth counsel by words without knowledge?' Job 38-2," quoth the constable. But he turned and made off with a majestic pace, his staff beating each step.

While it was obvious the woman had been stabbed to death, Creasy was only too glad to be rid of Phillymort. He made no objection when the taverner got up to fetch two cups of ale. The amber liquid soothed his parched throat and jangled nerves. It was a wonder the constable hadn't arrested him for the murder. Creasy recalled the note in his pocket as he swallowed a long draught of ale. He snorted ale through his nose and choked. The taverner pounded him upon the back.

"If the constable catches me I'm in for a scold," he said.

"A drop of my good ale never hurt anyone," the taverner said.

"O woe to ye hypocrites. Ye imbibers of the grape…" Creasy mocked the constable. He sucked in his cheeks, drew his brows into a scowl and pounded upon the table with his mug. Ale sloshed over the sides.

The taverner guffawed.

"Behold the drunkard in all his glory. Phillymort two: verse seven."

Creasy joined the taverner in mirth, laughing until tears came into his eyes.

"What are you doing?"

The cold voice froze the two men in their seats.

"Is this seemly?"

"No, Ma'am."

"Do you make fun of the dead?"

"No, Ma'am."

Creasy looked up. "We were making fun of Constable Philly-mort," he said.

"Oh. That's all right, then." Hetty Henry untied the strings of her hood and swept it off her head. "A taste of that ale wouldn't come amiss," she said. "It's cold out there." She spread out her cloak and seated herself on the bench next to Creasy. "More to the point, how do you come to be in a tavern past midnight with a dead woman, Increase Cotton? You'd better tell me all about it so I'll know how to help you."

FOURTEEN

The Ferretina woke me, saying merely that her brother must speak to me. I threw a nightrobe over my shift and ran down the stairs in my nightcap. I lead both the Ferretina and the Ferret into the kitchen where I fed them with slices of bread and butter and cups of cider that I warmed in a pot over the embers of the banked fire. Only after the Ferret's red nose warmed to pink did I grill my spy. "I followed Mister Cotton, like you said, Hetty. Well, most of the day it wasn't nothin' but standin' around waitin' for him to come out of his house. Come night I give up an' snuggled down on the top step. If anyone tries to sneak in they'd have to step on me. I never figured it'd be Mister Cotton who come out from inside. A good thing, too, I heard the door creak open an' fell off the step into the bushes. Oh, I hear the watchman call out the hour and it's midnight, I tell you. I follow him across the Green and down to Cody's tavern. He goes off to the back and I hear him holler at the top of his lungs, 'Murder!' he hollers an' I come runnin' back here. I didn't stay to see no murder." The boy's thin frame shivered.

I leaped up. "Was he hurt?" My innards turned to stone at the thought my friend might be even now dead upon the ground.

"No, Ma'am." The Ferret shook his shaggy head with vigor. "I could hear him hollerin' and poundin' upon the tavern door fit to bust it down." The Ferret twisted his cup around and around as he spoke.

"You've done well, Fer… Eliphalet."

The Ferretina stared at her sibling with pride. I directed her to set up a cot next to the hearth so he could get some well-earned sleep while I went back to my room to dress. Within ten minutes the Ferret was snoring and I let myself out for the trip to Cody's tavern. I carried a lantern for companion and managed to reach my destination without encountering the Watch. I did not want nor need to be interrogated by a doddering old man while Creasy was in trouble.

Trouble, did I think? I walked in to the tavern to the sounds of hilarity, an unseemly sound in the presence of death. I advanced and upbraided the men but since they were only laughing at the constable—Phillymort was a fool, there was no denying it—I joined them in a mug of ale. The cold was soon banished from my bones. I turned to the taverner, ignoring the dead woman behind me for the moment.

"Who is she?"

"My serving girl, that's who she is—was. Poor Pammie."

"Why would anyone want to kill her?" I asked.

The taverner shook his head. "I can't think of anyone had a grudge against her, Ma'am."

"Hetty," I said. "Hetty Henry. I'm a friend of Creasy's—Mister Cotton, here."

"She's good at solving murders." Creasy nodded with the wise look of a slightly befuddled owl.

"But who is she? How does she come to be here?"

The taverner scratched his head. "Her name's Pammie. Pamela Charlotte. I don't know much about her, but she's a good serving girl and quick. The best I've had. She just come in one day when it was real crowded and only me to see to everybody, an' she grabbed a tray and started right in to serve. I hired her on the spot. Customers took to her right off. Oh, she brought 'em in, such a pretty thing as she was. Now who woulda' done this to her?" The taverner took out a square of linen from beneath his smock and blew his nose.

I wondered if he'd miss the custom or the lady more. Setting down my empty glass, I stood to take a look at the redoubtable girl. I knew of no family named Charlotte, and I knew many people in the Town, what with my commercial ventures. I would spread the word, asking for information until my connections came through.

She was dressed in a robe of seagreen over a green-striped petticoat. The robe was low cut with a ruching of lace that barely concealed tiny bosoms. The dress was secondhand, but that was of no account, since clothing is dear and passed down from one generation to the next. Her features were unremarkable, pretty in a faded sort of way. Wisps of pale blonde hair stuck out from beneath a lace cap and eyes of mild blue stared unseeing up at the beams of the tavern. I was tempted to close the eyes of the poor girl but I thought the coroner might object to my interference.

I walked around the table inspecting the body. I noted the bloodied slits in the cloth of her robe where she had been stabbed in her midsection. The lady had been attacked with great savagery. Her arms bore slashes where she had tried to fend off the knife. Her hands were curled into fists. I spied something in her left fist, glanced at the two men who were busy drinking their ale, and pried it with care from the cold fingers. It proved to be a scrap of lace. I tucked it into my petticoat waist. There were no gaps in the lace that trimmed her dress so I must assume she'd torn it from her attacker. Now, lace might be found on the garments of either man or woman, but it was a place to start. I doubted that neither the coroner nor the constable would even notice a scrap of lace so I had no qualms about walking off with my prize.

With the pounding of the constable's staff upon the tavern door the taverner quickly collected the three mugs and hurried off to the grated bar with them. With the entry of the two men I took my leave. I was aware of Creasy's pleading eyes upon my back but he'd just have to put up with Constable Phillymort by himself. I resolved to post his bail should he be arrested. That was all I could do for him at the moment. Meanwhile, after a good night's sleep, I would make my plans for the next day. I am not one of those tortured souls who let a problem take over their nocturnal habits and who toss and turn all night long, but there were a few questions I could not help but consider as I walked home. Creasy received a note that took him to Cody's tavern. What was the purpose of the note? Was it an attempt to entrap Creasy as Jacob Joyliffe had been trapped? Could the killer be after the ministers of Boston, trying to ruin their reputations, as Cousin Cotton Mather suggested? I found that thought distasteful. I do not like to encourage Cousin Cotton in his bouts of nervous prostration, but in this case he might be correct. I put my questions aside as I lowered my head, drew my cape tightly about me, and soldiered on against a harbor wind with a bite like a shark. At this point all I wanted was the warmth of my bed.

Next morning I rose at my usual hour of six o'clock, dressed with some care for I was to meet Alexandre at mid-day, and sent out for a breakfast of ham, eggs, toast and a pot of chocolate. I tried not to waken the Ferret, who'd been up all night, but the aroma of warm ham slices did the trick. He and his sister joined me for the morning repast.

"Meat for breakfast?" The Ferret shook his shaggy head in wonder as he eyed the ham much as a wolf eyes a lost lamb. He grabbed a hearty helping of the meat, smeared his toast with preserves made from my own fruit trees, emptied half the platter of eggs and shoveled it all down as fast as he could. The Ferretina nudged him to mind his manners but her brother only sniffed.

"Hetty don't care. She knows I'm a growin' boy."

"You'll grow as fat as Priscilla, my prize pig, if you keep on like that," I said.

But I remembered hard times when I was a youngster and tempered my lecture with a smile. I poured mugs of chocolate for each of us.

The Ferret drank his down with a sigh of contentment. "That was purely good, Hetty." He regarded me with sharp eyes. "Who was that dead body last night? I didn't stay to look."

The Ferretina sneaked a peak at me from the corner of her

eye. She'd fallen asleep waiting for me. I'd left her in the chair rather than waken her, but she must have managed to stagger to the little cot I'd set up for her in what was meant to be the birthing room.

"It was a woman. A serving girl at Cody's tavern over by the Common. Pamela Charlotte was her name. Do you know of her?"

Both young people shook their heads.

"I couldn't see if 'twas man or woman last night. I just thought you'd want to know about it, that's all." The Ferret scratched his shaggy head. "We don't get out that way much."

The inference was that the Common where Boston citizens once grazed their cows, was above their touch. That wasn't meant to be, and I vowed to take them to the next fair or to the next training session of the militia so they could see the tents, nibble on gingerbread and watch the companies march back and forth across the green like any other citizen of the Town.

"You want me to keep on followin' Mister Creasy?" The Ferret raised thin brows in question.

"Yes. The danger hasn't lessened. In fact, I'm afraid it's stronger now." Creasy would raise heaven and earth to find the killer of Pamela Charlotte. It wouldn't matter that she was only a serving girl. No matter how humble her station, the young woman deserved justice. I agreed with that sentiment. Her murderer must be caught and punished. And I wanted to know why the victim had singled Creasy out with a note. Why him, and not the constable? Well, knowing Constable Phillymort I could understand. Still, there were other magistrates and other ministers, although Creasy certainly had a soft spot for a damsel in distress. And he was the only one who doubted the guilt of Jacob Joyliffe in the murder of the fencing master. Could there be a connection between the two murders? Perkney's women were all married, or so it had seemed. Still, Pamela Charlotte seemed a reasonably attractive woman in death so she might have been quite presentable in life. One could never tell with men.

I turned my attention to the Ferret. "Keep your eyes and ears open for any information about Pamela Charlotte, too. People are bound to talk of the murder and I want every scrap of information about her I can get. I think she's the key to the dancing master's murder."

I dismissed the boy and issued instructions to his sister, who asked to earn her keep by cleaning or doing such errands as I commissioned. The Ferretina began immediately with the clean up of our breakfast repast. I liked a girl with initiative.

In my office at the warehouse I consulted with my clerk, approved invoices and in general busied myself with work. Running a mercantile business takes many hours of labor, even though I hire adequate help. My tasks accomplished, I set out for my seamstress, the scrap of lace I'd found upon the corpse tucked inside my bosom. She, however, had never seen such a fine kind of work before, which she thought to be of Flemish design. Here I'd assumed I'd held a clue to the identity of the man guilty of two murders. I thought of the exquisite laces worn at the throats and sleeves of my many male friends and not a one of them wore anything like this. My spirits were a trifle dampened by this setback, but I vowed not to let them show to my charming new acquaintance. In this I was not successful, for my host was quite perceptive.

Alexandre guessed my mood. He reached across the table and laid his long, tapered fingers over mine.

"Is something troubling you?" he asked.

We'd just devoured bowls of fish chowder, shared a plump duck and consumed stewed pumpkins, pickled walnuts, cheese, and dried apple pie.

Perhaps the sweet concern he showed to me and the flutter in my groin made me sharper than I meant to be. I withdrew my hand a trifle abruptly. "Of course something is troubling me. Two murders are troubling me." As indeed they were. Creasy says when I get something in my head I am like a dog with a bone. I won't let go.

"You believe that the two deaths are connected, my friend

Francis and the young woman found upon the Common?" Two perfect brows arched in concern. "Is this what the constable thinks?"

"Our constable is not capable of thought," While that was true, I knew I should show respect for the office. To make up for my poor manners I added in a softened tone, "I have found what I believe to be a clue. It's a scrap of lace I discovered in the dead woman's hand. I thought perhaps my seamstress could identify it—even tell me who has purchased this kind of lace—but she could not."

"Ah… May I see it?" He held out his long fingers.

"Are you a connoisseur of women's laces?" I spoke in a light tone and raised my own brows at him in challenge. It would not have surprised me if my handsome friend knew a great deal about women's dress, or undress. I pictured him unlacing the strings of my own gown and felt my limbs tremble. In haste I produced the little scrap of lace and handed it to him for inspection, taking care that my fingers should not touch his. I really must control myself. The attraction I felt for the man was distracting me from my duty.

Alexandre gave the scrap a brief look. "You know that the lace-makers of Belgium fled with us to London? I know an old woman, a Flemish lace-maker. She may be able to identify this lace. Shall we go visit her?"

I rose from the bench. "May we go now?"

The old woman knew the lace, the lace-maker in London and the name of the ship that carried it to the Boston market. The captain of the ship was none other than the husband of my own friend, Sarah Welsteed. I must have shown my surprise at the mention of the captain's name.

Alexandre took my hand within his as we left the old woman. "What shall we do now?"

I assumed a casual air, an emotion I was far from feeling. "Oh, the wife of the captain is a friend of mine. I'll call upon her on my way home. Perhaps she can tell me who purchased the lace. She keeps the captain's books, you see." I withdrew my hand from his grasp, but I did so gently. I did not mean to discourage the gentleman, after all.

"Hetty. You won't put yourself in danger, will you?" He looked down at me, his gray eyes serious with concern.

At that I chuckled. Sarah Welsteed was as dangerous as a newborn babe. "Mistress Welsteed has a little son with a broken leg and three other children to care for. I know she cannot possibly have murdered anyone. It is not in her nature, for one thing. For another, her time has been accounted for since your partner's death."

"Even so, may I accompany you?"

"No. Really, Alexandre, that is quite unnecessary." I dismissed him with good humor, touched that he concerned himself with my safety, but I knew I was as safe as a lamb with a shepherd standing guard in Sarah's presence. I placated him by promising to send him a note upon my return.

I giggled to myself all the way to the Welsteed household. Sweet Sarah Welsteed a bloody murderer? She had such a soft nature that she would not consent to have the little chicks she'd raised into hens slaughtered for the family dinner table. As a result her yard was full of poultry. One tripped over them on the doorstep, indeed, as I nearly did now. The hen squawked and feathers flew as I kicked it out of the way.

The quiet I met upon my entrance into the house was a trifle unnerving. Sarah came to greet me after a wait of several minutes. She explained that they had carried little Tom outside and settled him on a bench beneath an apple tree with orders for the other children to entertain him. The day being a pleasant one and the little boy wrapped up well, Sarah felt a change of scenery would improve the boy's spirits. I knew it would do me good, for I'd have a chance to talk to Sarah without the usual spate of screaming brats. Not that I dislike children, mind, but I prefer them disciplined and quiet in my presence. I had reason to know that children are quite intelligent and trustworthy when set to a task. The problem with Sarah is that she doesn't know how to control her brood.

Sarah settled herself upon a high backed bench, her sewing spread around her, while I took the chair opposite.

"How cozy this is, just the two of us settled in for a chat." Sarah gave a sigh of content. "I've had little time to myself since my poor boy's accident. How kind of you to call, Hetty. I'm sorry about the other day. We didn't really get to talk, did we?" She picked through a pile of cloth and pulled out a dove-colored dress, which she spread across her lap. A needle and thread were stuck into the collar of the robe. She slipped the needle out. Sarah looked up at me. "Have you discovered who murdered poor Francis?"

I shook my head. "Not yet."

"Well, I know how talented you are at detecting wrongdoing, Hetty. You've had very real successes at it. I'm sure you'll bring his killer to justice. Indeed, we must all hope for it." Sarah threaded a needle with silk string as she spoke.

"Yes, but I don't feel so confident just now. There has been another murder, you know."

Sarah nodded. "The girl on the Common. It's what everyone talks of, you know. But what she has to do with Francis I cannot even imagine."

"Sarah, you knew the man. Would he have courted a tavern serving-girl?" I leaned forward for her answer. She was the only woman I trusted to tell me the truth of the matter.

"So… You do think the two deaths are connected?" Sarah spoke with slow consideration. "Who can say with men? I should say that he appeared to be very much the gentleman, with a taste for those things a gentleman favors. While he might be acquainted with a serving girl I doubt very much that she would appeal to him as a woman. Oh, dear. I don't mean to sound so disapproving. The poor girl. Who am I to judge her?"

I heard the genuine note of distress in her voice. "I'm sure you wish to see justice done for both murders, Sarah, as must we all. It helps me to learn whatever little I can about both the victims."

"To be sure. Ask me anything you wish. I shall answer to the best of my ability." She lifted her head with a brave look for me. Then she turned to her sewing. Her needle was threaded with a fine silk string. She lifted the arm of the robe and her needle flashed back and forth like a tiny sliver of silver.

"What is that you are darning?" I leaned forward for a better look.

"It's my sister's sleeve. You know Eliza, my husband's sister. She tore it on a nail. The lace caught upon it. Eliza can be quite careless of her appearance sometimes. I despair of her. I know she would like a husband but she will ignore a rip or a tear or a spot. That does not appeal to a man."

"Where did she get the lace?" I tried to keep my voice steady. The lace of the woman's sleeve looked oddly familiar. I felt a sickening in my innards. There are times when one would rather not have one's suspicions confirmed. My hand went to my bosom, where I'd tucked the scrap of lace. Of course, other people may have bought the same lace. That is what I'd come to ask the woman, after all.

"Why, the captain brought me several yards of it. He bought it in London on his last voyage. Eliza and I have trimmed several of our robes with it." She lifted the sleeve and I could see the hole ripped from an edge. "I insisted upon repairing this for her. It's the least I can do. Eliza is so good to us. I could not manage the children without her, what with poor Tom's broken leg and all. It's a blessing that she has come to stay with us."

"Oh," I found myself wondering what to say next, and nearly stammered when I asked the question. "When did she rip her sleeve?" I'm sure I held my breath for her reply.

"Oh, I'm not sure as to that, but I spotted it upon her bed this morning. I just picked it up and insisted upon mending it for her. I told her it was no trouble, and the very least I could do."

"Did your sister-in-law leave the house last night?" I asked.

"Oh, I shouldn't think so. She sits up with Tom, poor boy. His pain is worse at night, although he did say he slept well for the first time since the accident. The doctor left a draught for him and it seems the draught finally took effect." Sarah went on with her mending. "I sleep the night through, thanks to Eliza. Why, she—"

I interrupted her with a request for a cup of chocolate. "My throat is a trifle dry."

Sarah set aside her sewing and jumped up directly for the kitchen.

As soon as she left the room I pulled out my scrap of lace and compared it to the torn sleeve. It fit well within the ragged edge. My innards roiled with upset. I forced myself to take deep breaths. When Sarah returned with a tray I had settled back in my seat, but I needed the calming warmth of the chocolate, which she served in tiny china cups. I sipped at mine, upbraiding myself for my haste in judgment just because the woman tore her sleeve. Well, others could have done the same, man or woman. Men wore bands of lace and lace trimmed their sleeves. A torn sleeve was hardly proof that Eliza Welsteed was a murderess. Besides, she was sitting up with a sick child. She would not leave a sick child under her care, would she? I thought of one more question as I set down my little cup.

"Did your sister-in-law accompany you to your dancing lessons?" The question hinted at the need for a chaperone.

"Oh, no." Sarah's face grew pale. "She did not approve of my lessons with Francis. She gave me a great scold every time I went. Eliza stayed home with the children. I'm afraid I told her untruths, that I was going to the shops or to visit a friend, and I changed the times of our meetings to fool her. It was silly of me, but I did." From pale, her skin turned a rosy pink.

I'd seen Sarah's sister-in-law at the dinner party and I could sympathize with my friend. Eliza Welsteed was a tall, bold-eyed woman with large, awkward hands and a scornful countenance. She shared her height with her brother but seemed to have none of his bluff good nature. Could Eliza have followed Sarah to discover how she spent her time? Even if she had not, she could easily have found out Perkney's address. But where would she have met

Pamela Charlotte? Surely she would not frequent Cody's tavern, although she might have gone in to dine with a party of family or friends. A visit to see blind Henry was in order. Perhaps he could tell me if Eliza Welsteed had appeared in Perkney's rooms.

Henry, however, had no notion of the woman. As I described Eliza Welsteed he shook his head. His little girl stood behind him. She jerked at his coat.

"What is it, Libby?" Henry put out his hand, resting it on the child's curly head. He gave her a fond smile.

"Excuse me, Papa," the child lisped. "I have seen the black lady."

"Did you, my love?" Henry cocked his head.

"Yes, Sir. When mama sent me to fetch you home."

"Where did you see her?" I knelt as I spoke. Two bright black eyes sparkled into mine.

The child placed a tiny finger into her rosebud mouth. "Standing in the road just outside where Papa used to fiddle for the fine ladies. I saw her there. She was so tall and she had big hands and she was dressed all in black." The child's voice was firm.

I smiled at the child and dug into my pocket for a coin. A seven-year-old child placed Eliza Welsteed at the scene where the murder of the dancing master took place. It was hardly impressive testimony for a magistrate, but at least it was something for me to go on. The child accepted the coin with quiet gravity. I was about to rise when another question occurred to me. "Did you ever see a pretty blonde lady, about my size, standing out there with the black lady?"

"No, Ma'am."

My hopes sank within me at this solemn reply.

"She wasn't with the black lady. That's the lady with the basket. There were right good smells coming from that basket. It made me hungry for my dinner. But I never saw her with the black lady."

What a bright child. I told Henry as much as I stood and faced him. Libby put both women at the scene. Here was the connection. Pamela might well have brought a dinner from the tavern over to the dancing master. I must check with the taverner, but it certainly seemed possible. And it was possible that Pamela had seen Eliza Welsteed on the day Perkney was murdered. Poor Jacob Joyliffe. His argument with the dancing master was ill timed. Now here was information that could prove his innocence. If only I could obtain the evidence I needed to clear the poor man. And tall as she was, would Eiza Welsteed be capable of knocking down my old Samuel? Well, perhaps. She had those big hands, after all. But why look for Perkney's ledger? And why at my warehouse? Was her name in Perkney's ledger? That seemed doubtful. Of course, she might want to erase Sarah's name, thinking to protect her. Would the woman kill for that? It was time to consult Mister Increase Cotton. As a minister perhaps he could shed some light upon the guilty secrets of this human soul.

FIFTEEN

One thing I will admit about Creasy—he bears me no jealous feelings when I find a piece of information that he himself has not discovered. His vanity is not upset by my success, whether in a business sense or in our investigations together. In that way we make a harmonious team. I showed him the scrap of lace from Eliza's dress and asked his advice on how to confront Eliza Welsteed on her perversity. I knew he had admired the lady, but he did me the justice of believing in my conviction that I'd found the killer.

"I was hoping it was that Rufus Catesby, but I inquired and he was in jail at the time of Perkney's death," he said with a sigh. "It's difficult to believe a lady could commit such horrors.

"Just don't go confronting her by yourself, Hetty. It must be a public confession," Creasy said. "She's not a member of my church. I believe she is a member of good Mister Willard's congregation. Perhaps Mister Willard will be able to convince her that she should confess her sin."

"Well she's not going to make a public confession of murder or she would have done so by now. What I need is for you to be a witness. You'll make an excellent witness should she confess to me. And I think I know how to get her to confess." I outlined my plan, and with a suggestion and a sigh or two, Creasy agreed to be a part of it.

"But not behind the tavern," he said, with a stern look at me. "She could get at you too easily there. Try the burial ground behind

Mister Willard's church. If she's going to confess at all, that may be the place to confront her. I can hide behind a tombstone. You can at least put a stone or two between you for some protection. Remember, we believe she may have killed two people. She will not hesitate to attack you, Hetty. You must be on your guard, and I must be close by to help you."

I was well aware of the danger and counted upon Creasy to bring some rope to bind the woman. Between us we created and penned an unsigned note and sent it off to Eliza Wellsteed setting the next night at midnight for an interview in the burial ground. So that she would take the note seriously I demanded fifty pounds for my silence as to what I knew concerning the death of Pamela Charlotte. I signed the note from: A Friend of Pamela C.

I spent the next day cursing myself for my foolhardiness. To take my mind off my folly I accepted an invitation to take supper with Alexandre Bernon. If anyone could distract me it would be Alexandre. I thought of his long mouth and his arched nose and those intriguing gray eyes. Yes, a distraction indeed. We shared a pleasant supper of bread, meat and cheese at a tavern near the wharf where his rooms were located. These were the same rooms where poor Perkney was killed. That thought proved unnerving, so I banished it from my mind with resolution. I did not want to think of the chore that faced me, either. All I wished was to do was to enjoy the company of a man whom I admired and with whom I could converse on topics that had nothing to do with questions of the law or justice or taking the life of another human being. He succeeded in entertaining me to such an extent that I nearly took a third glass of wine. I refused, knowing I must keep a clear head for my midnight meeting. When Alexandre pressed me to come to his rooms I refused that invitation as well. I had another meeting in mind, one not nearly so pleasurable. Oh, the tasks that duty impresses upon me. I left Alexandre seated at the table and strode forth upon my destiny.

After a few sighs that frosted in the brisk night air I concentrated upon my plan to confront a killer. Creasy met me by the round marsh where the chorus of lusty young frogs nearly drowned out my greeting. We cut across the common together. The sentry tower stood skeletal in outline against the dark sky, ready to warn Boston's citizens of attack by a foreign force. I wished it were lit like a beacon. We did not speak. I was depressed by what I was about to face, although I kept my brain busy going over the speech I had planned. The contrast between the pleasant company I'd just left and the task ahead no doubt influenced my mood.

Creasy kept well behind me as I walked into the old graveyard behind Mister Willard's church. I turned my head in time to see the man duck behind a tombstone. It was some consolation to know he was there. I took up my place, a tombstone before me and other stones beside me. The poor founders of the town were buried here. Little did they know or little approve of the use I'd put to their final resting places. Still, it was private but it was also a public spot in the heart of Boston, which was patrolled by the night watch. The stones seemed woefully small now that I depended upon their protection. I shivered from the crisp night air and pulled the hood of my cloak up to conceal my face. She must not recognize me before she confessed. She would not believe Mrs. Hetty Henry, rich widow, would dun her for fifty pounds, surely a large sum to her but she'd know it wasn't such a huge sum to me.

Shifting from foot to foot I waited. While I don't consider myself as a coward, the thought of the two murders I believed Eliza Welsteed had committed kept my nerves on edge. Knowing Creasy was near gave me some comfort. At least there would be a witness to the confession…if I succeeded in getting one. I caught my breath when a hooded figure materialized out of the night. It seemed to float among the tombstones like an uneasy spirit. I leaned my knees tight up against the stone before me for support. The feel of the hard stone through my cloak had the effect of straightening my backbone, physically and mentally. I could not see her face, but I had the advantage of knowing it was Eliza

Welsteed. My hand reached down inside my cloak to touch the small knife I'd belted upon my hip.

Eliza made no greeting. She held out a bag. "Here is the money you requested. Take it."

I made no move. If she thought I was going to get near her, she was much mistaken.

She jiggled the bag so the coins clanked inside it. "Take it," she said, her voice hard.

"Place it on top of the stone before you," I said, lowering my own voice in disguise.

Eliza set the bag upon the tombstone. I heard the chink of coins, yet I knew she kept her hand upon the bag.

"Let go of it," I said. She could easily swing it as a weapon.

She released the bag.

"Who are you?" Eliza Welsteed hissed the question like the serpent she was. She leaned forward to peer at my face.

"One who would see justice done for the murders of Francis Perkney and Pamela Charlotte." I spoke the words before I thought. I was supposed to be here for payment, not for honor.

"The strumpet and the whoreson." Her shrill voice cut through the night air.

"What had either of them done to you to deserve murder, a poor tavern wench and a dancing master." The indignation I felt at her callous contempt I could not conceal in my voice. Surely there was a reason for her hatred of the two.

"A poor tavern wench who demanded money for her silence. Like you." Eliza Welsteed spit out her venom at me. "She saw me coming out of Master Perkney's rooms that day and followed me to my brother's house. She said she noted my distress and wanted to help. Yes, help herself to my brother's money. That's what the slattern wanted."

"So you agreed to meet her behind the tavern and stabbed her to death." I kept my voice as low and calm as I could.

"The strumpet deserved to die, the fornicator, the Whore of Babylon!" Eliza Welsteed's voice rang harsh with contempt.

"Why Perkney? What had he done to you? Were you one of his conquests?" I was curious. Eliza Welsteed did not appear to have anything in common with the ladies Perkney chose for dalliance.

"I? Demean myself with the likes of the dancing master?" Eliza spoke in coarse indignation. "I should hope I have more respect for my soul than that. No. That one preferred married ladies. He took advantage of them. My brother's own wife..." She paused. "I begged him to leave her alone, that my brother was not here to protect her reputation, that he took advantage of her sweet and trusting nature, but he only laughed. He mocked me. He said oh such nasty things of poor Sarah. He told me the indecent acts he perpetrated upon her, and I was just a jealous old hag—that's what he called me. I could not stand to hear such things. I reached out to the wall to steady myself. I didn't mean to kill him, I just reached out and there was a foil to hand. I ran the man through. He did not expect it. No indeed, he did not expect it. I never thought..." Her voice faltered.

"Why did you not go to the magistrate and confess your act? You might have pleaded self-defense or great provocation. Why let poor Jacob Joyliffe be arrested for your crime?"

"That worm." Her disgust of the poor man was obvious. "I doubt he will be hung. He has the protection of the ministers in this town. Why should you care?" Eliza Welsteed took a step nearer. "You've your blood money for your silence." As she spoke, she reached out and knocked the bag of coins to the ground. The coins tumbled out with clinks and dull thuds.

I believe she expected me to bend down to pick them up. I stepped back. She lunged at me. I caught a glimpse of something sharp and shining in her hand as I jerked away from her.

I did not wait around for rescue, I ran for my life, hollering, "Help. Help!" Fear lent me wings.

From the corner of my eyes I saw Creasy rise up from behind a tombstone and just as quickly drop to the ground with a groan. I had my own little knife in my hand at that point, but it seemed as useless as a dining fork against a pitchfork. I made for the gate, dodging tombstones as I ran. I'd left the gate ajar for just such an exit.

The sounds of a scuffle came to my ears but I did not turn until I'd flown through the gate and slammed it shut. I shot the bolt, still screaming for help. Where oh where was the watchman? I hoped Creasy had managed to capture the vile witch. I peered through the bars. What if she managed to escape? Eliza could climb over the fence, I supposed, but I'd have flown the coop by the time she reached the gate. I turned my head this way and that looking for the watch as I continued to shout, adding "Ho. Murder!" to my cries.

In the distance I spotted a light jogging up and down. Someone must have heard me. Relief flowed through me like a creek after a downpour of rain. "This way," I called. "The burial ground." Shadowy figures appeared behind the fence, advancing upon me. "Hurry." I turned toward the light, which proved to be the lantern of the watchman. I wasn't taking any chances. Whether Creasy had Eliza captive or Eliza dragged Creasy in her wake, I was ready to run.

The watchman reached me, held up his lantern high and by its glare I made out three figures approaching before me across the burial ground. Three? One was clearly a woman struggling in the grasp of a man, but who was the man? I spotted Creasy limping behind the other two. "Creasy," I called out, concerned lest he had injured himself on my behalf. As the little group approached the gate the watchman unbarred it and thrust it open.

"Mister Cotton?" the watchman called out, recognizing the minister. "Are you hurt, Sir?"

"That woman's a confessed murderess," I said to the watchman. "Mister Cotton will confirm it." I gasped as the figures reached the gate, for Alexandre Bernon held the tall, struggling woman, whose arms were pinioned behind her back and tied with stout rope.

"We must get this woman to the magistrate at once," Creasy spoke to the watchman.

I touched Alexandre's sleeve as he passed me, too overcome with surprise to speak. He held a firm grip upon Eliza Welsteed's bound arms. The woman glared at me, baring her teeth like a rabid dog. She hissed something but I could not make out the words.

We made a curious procession marching through the darkened streets, the watchman providing the only light as he led us, his lantern held high. At the magistrate's house he set the lantern upon the step and used his staff to bang upon the door. The sound echoed through the black streets. A dim light appeared in an upstairs window as we waited. While it seemed like an eternity, it was only a matter of minutes before the door was opened to us by Mister Floyd, his banyan of scarlet silk wrapped firmly about his portly person and his wig askew. We were greeted with remarkable restraint, I thought, under the circumstances. The magistrate led us to his study where we crowded in, the lady in captivity become sullen and silent. Creasy told our tale of confronting the murderess while he witnessed, and of the Huguenot gentleman's help in the capture. Alexandre shrugged one broad shoulder, insisting he'd only helped Mister Cotton to confine the murderess. I kept silent, for once in my life, only nodding when the magistrate asked for my confirmation. Mister Floyd sent the watchman off to fetch the constable to take Mistress Welsteed to the Boston jail.

While we waited for the constable to arrive I addressed Eliza Welsteed. "Was it you who ransacked my warehouse office? And tied up my watchman?"

She bared her teeth at me but remained silent. I repeated the question, adding, "What rogues did you hire for your dirty work?" I did not mean for the rogues to go unpunished. Let them meddle in my business affairs at their peril.

"Do you think me incapable of hitting an old man on the head with a bottle? I was in a hurry, lest you come back and find me there. I should have treated you the same as I treated yon minister. He interrupted me at my task and I hit him, as well. I wanted to find that ledger."

"You were after the ledger? Why—what was it to you?" I found it hard to believe a woman could attack a man. With an old man like Samuel, perhaps she might find success, but one as young and strong as Creasy? Of course upon inspection, she was taller than Creasy, who was of average height, and her hands were big and capable. By surprise she might succeed.

"The name, of course. To protect my brother's good name. I didn't think of it until after... I could not think clearly after Master Perkney's death. That was an accident, Sir." She turned to the magistrate with an earnest demeanor. She addressed him, disregarding me. "Only later had I bethought the dancing master must have a record of his clients and Sarah's name would be on it. Who knew what lewd references he might write about her. Poor, foolish Sarah. What troubles her deviant behavior has wrought upon us all."

"It wasn't Sarah's deviant behavior that has you before the magistrate," I said. I couldn't help myself. Her attempt to blame Sarah when the woman had murdered two people made me indignant. Another patronizing voice interrupted any further confrontation.

"'Therefore will I stretch out my hand against thee and destroy thee.' Jeremiah fifteen-six." Mister Phillymont the Constable stalked into the room, his staff pounding upon the floor. He addressed me with his words, as if I were the guilty party here. I gestured to my friends and rose. Let Mister Floyd complete the charges. I was glad to leave the woman to the unmerciful care of Constable Phillymort. Indeed, I could almost feel sorry for her.

Within the hour Creasy, Alexandre and I were safely ensconced in my own little office on Henry's Wharf. I produced a bottle of good French brandy and three glass tumblers. I had my own means of procuring fine goods.

"What happened, Creasy? I saw you go down. And you, Alexandre. I was never more surprised in my life to see you at that gate. How did you know?"

Creasy answered first. "I tripped over a child's tombstone. I hit my head and was a little dazed, that's why I couldn't imme- diately come to your rescue. I'm sorry." He bent over to rub his shin. I noticed a black streak of dirt across the white stocking.

"Alexandre?" I turned to that handsome gentleman.

He sipped at his tumbler, turning it in his long fingers and admiring the liquid within. "This is good."

I titled my head, waiting for an answer. His eyes sparkled like gray stars. I tried not to get distracted.

Alexandre grinned. "You were so unresponsive at dinner, so distracted that I thought you must be up to some mischief. I fol- lowed you. It was rather foolhardy of you to face a murderess on your own, you know, but when I noticed Mister Cotton following as well, I knew you'd been wise enough to bring someone with you. That relieved me a great deal, I must say. I thought I would just observe and assist if needed."

I reached out and touched his free hand, which lay upon the desk before me. "Well, I'm glad you were there."

Creasy set his glass down with care. He raised a hand to his forehead with a gingerly touch. "I couldn't help it. I tripped."

I noticed a red bump there by his right forehead. Poor Creasy. He'd suffered for my sake, and that was brave of him. "But you heard her confession." I wanted to mollify him. "You are a wit- ness to what she said, Creasy, and what she tried to do to me. With you as a witness there will be no question of her guilt. I'm heartily grateful for that, my friend. You have no idea what com- fort your presence gave me. I shall drink to the health of both of you," I said, raising my glass tumbler.

The brandy warmed my shivering body. It slid down through my throat with the fire of liquid coals. All of a sudden I felt as though I'd been hit over the head by an iron forge. The weight of the tension I'd held in for the entire evening collapsed upon me. All I craved was my bed in my rooms above, to sleep in solitary silence. And I meant in solitary silence. I attempted to be polite and listen to the tales the two men were sharing, biding fair to be a rivalry for my interest, but it would not do. I realized Alexandre expected to share my bed for the night and that Creasy had every intention of stalling that intention, but I could not play their little game. I drained my glass, set it upon the desk and rose.

"Gentlemen. Enjoy the brandy as long as you wish. Samuel will lock up behind you. The night's events have exhausted me, I'm afraid. I'm for sleep." I left the room without bothering to look back.

ABOUT AUTHOR M.E. KEMP

M. E. Kemp was born in Oxford, MA, a town her ancestors settled in 1713. With her Grandmother's tales of family adventures and her father's interest in American history, Kemp became an avid fan of New England's colonial history, writing a prize-winning short story in middle school and continuing with articles that appeared in national magazines. She writes a current series of historical mystery novels featuring two nosy Puritans as detectives. She is married to Jack H. Rothstein and lives in Saratoga Springs, site of many of her short stories concerning the Revolutionary War Battle of Saratoga. Her two kitties, Boris and Natasha, often reenact that battle for her.

Check out Kemp's work at: www.mekempmysteries.com

Breinigsville, PA USA
28 November 2010
250212BV00006B/1/P